SHADOW

Geoffrey Trease's lin[...] success of his first b[...] (1934). The book intr[...] to children's literature, portraying Robin Hood as a revolutionary leading his outlaws in a fight against class oppression. Many thousands of copies were sold in the Soviet Union and the author was invited to visit the country. "I lived in Russia from May to October during 1935," he says, "and I've used the knowledge picked up in my subsequent books, both historical ones and those dealing with modern Russia." The most recent of these books, his ninety-ninth, is *Shadow under the Sea*, set in the Yalta region of the present day – the time of Gorbachev, *glasnost* and *perestroika*.

The book's central character is a girl, Kate, but, as in most of Trease's novels, both sexes are well represented. Indeed, he was one of the first to write adventures in which girls and boys played an equal role. "When I started," he recalls, "girls were an inferior sort of species, and there were separate books for boys and girls which were demarcated rather like lavatories." He remembers returning from his trip to the Soviet Union and suggesting to an editor that he write an article about a mixed children's camp he'd attended. "Fine," said the editor, "but try not to mention the girls too much, will you?"

Born and brought up in Nottingham, near Sherwood Forest, Geoffrey Trease has written over forty adventure novels for young people – including the Walker titles *The Arpino Assignment* and *The Calabrian Quest* – as well as adult novels, plays, biographies and other works of non-fiction. He now lives in Bath.

Also by Geoffrey Trease

The Arpino Assignment
Bows Against the Barons
The Calabrian Quest
The Cormorant Venture
Cue for Treason
The Iron Tsar
No Boats on Bannermere
The Red Towers of Granada
Saraband for Shadows
This Is Your Century
The White Nights of St Petersburg

SHADOW UNDER THE SEA

GEOFFREY TREASE

WALKER BOOKS
LONDON

First published 1990 by Walker Books Ltd
87 Vauxhall Walk, London SE11 5HJ

This edition published 1991
Reprinted 1991

Text © 1990 Geoffrey Trease
Cover illustration © 1990 David Juniper

Printed and bound in Great Britain by
Cox and Wyman Ltd, Reading, Berkshire

British Library Cataloguing in Publication Data
Trease, Geoffrey
Shadow under the sea.
I. Title
823'.914 [F]
ISBN 0-7445-1450-9

Author's Note

Yalta is, of course, a real place. I spent two summer months there long ago. But Shulgin, like all the other characters, is imaginary. Although the Soviet Government and Press have exposed and punished many cases of crime and corruption in various parts of the country, I have no evidence of any such scandals in the region which is the setting of this story.

ONE

She must get rid of Olga.

In the past hour that had become brutally clear. At all costs she must get rid of Olga.

She viewed the necessity with reluctance, but her determination did not waver. Normally kind and easygoing, Kate could be ruthless when she had to be. With Olga, as she had realized with every minute that passed, only ruthlessness would work.

"And this is our invaluable Olga Petrovna!" Little Dr Yasnov had introduced them with, Kate now remembered, a slightly apologetic look in his shrewd grey eyes. "Olga will look after you – take you into the town, show you round, explain everything."

"How kind," Kate had said politely, "but I'd be quite all right on my own, honestly."

"We should not like you to get into difficulties." The Russian girl had thrust out a massive hand in greeting. "For foreigners there can be all kinds of difficulties. Is better I go with you, I think."

"Well . . . if it isn't too much trouble. . ."

"Is no trouble," said Olga firmly. There seemed no more to be said.

For the past week Kate had roamed freely round Moscow while her father was tied up in conference sessions. She had met with no problems, only friendliness. And surely down here in the far south among the holiday-makers, a thousand miles from the shadow of the Kremlin, she could not need an escort?

Still, one could not be rude. And it solved the question of transport into Yalta. Olga said that there was a truck going down, and led the way round to the kitchen entrance of the sanatorium.

"Excuse, please," she said, clambering up first. "Is better I sit beside the man." The driver grinned a welcome to Kate, flashing a row of metal-filled teeth, as she greeted him in Russian.

"Ah! You speak a little our language?" said Olga. She did not look as pleased as the driver.

"Just a little."

"Is good." Olga's tone was more grudging than approving. "Is better we speak English together. Then, what I show you, you understand good, yes? We have many visitors to our sanatorium. British, American, many countries. They say I have good accent. You think so? The practice makes perfect, yes?"

"You can say that again," Kate murmured, as the truck gathered speed down the winding drive.

It was practice she herself was looking forward to – but in Russian.

"The practice makes perfect," Olga repeated with plodding, painstaking enunciation. "Did I make an error the first time?"

"No – no, it was fine."

"Then why you ask me to say again?" the Russian girl demanded in an injured tone.

"I didn't mean – oh, forget it," said Kate wearily.

8

She longed, mischievously, to start a conversation with the driver and show that her own Russian was not too bad. But it was hard to talk across the substantial Olga wedged between them.

She would have been happy enough to enjoy the short journey in silence, taking in the scenery. She had only glimpsed it last night from the helicopter in the twenty-minute flight from Simferopol.

The scenery was really something. Who would have thought that this was still Russia? The endless monotonous plain with its cornfields and sunflowers had given place to dove-grey precipices and luxuriant subtropical trees. And when they swung round a bend the world fell away, and infinitely far below them the sea spread to the horizon.

Spiky palms, dark, pointed cypresses, vine-terraces, silvery olive trees . . . ornate gateways, snow-white mansions glimpsed behind curtains of greenery. . .

"Grand dukes and wealthy capitalists lived there before the Revolution," Olga explained. "Many are now sanatoria and holiday-homes – like ours. Is better, yes?"

"Oh, yes, definitely!"

Kate was all for sanatoria and good health services for everyone. But one part of her, fed by her reading of old Russian literature, felt a wistful regret for that vanished world.

Olga chattered on. "In this region are eighty sanatoria." Clearly she had a passion for facts

9

and figures, with, unfortunately, an unselfish desire to share them with other people, whether interested or not.

"What a lovely day!" Kate tried to stem the flow. "Like Italy."

"Yalta's hours of sunshine equal those of the Riviera. The mean annual temperature is —" The statistic was lost in the rattle of the truck. "One day – if Dr Yasnov give me the day off! – I take you to Nikitsky Botanic Garden. It covers five hundred hectares, it contains twenty-eight thousand different trees and plants. I show you!"

I bet you will, thought Kate despondently. Every one of the twenty-eight thousand.

Most decidedly she must get rid of Olga. Not for this had she come to Russia.

The girl was making propaganda speeches all the time. "This you do not have in the West!" she would cry exultantly. Kate would long to retort, "But we *do*!" But she soon realized that Olga's mind was as shut as her mouth was open.

They were descending into the outskirts of the town. The next bend showed the sea much closer beneath them. Bright-sailed yachts skimmed like giant butterflies. Launches cut white ruffles in their wake. There were surfers and swimmers and, along the pebbly beach, ranks of bronzed sunbathers laid out like sausages for some gigantic barbecue. Coloured umbrellas were dotted everywhere.

The truck could not drive along the seafront, so they were dropped in a shopping street close by. "We can return by taxi," said Olga.

They had stopped outside a big food store. A long line of harassed-looking women stood patiently waiting along the kerb. "Surely this isn't a queue?" Kate enquired wickedly. "I thought there were no shortages nowadays."

"I have no idea what they are waiting for," said Olga, rather edgily. "I hear a band in the distance. Perhaps they wait to see a procession."

The truck-driver must have guessed what they were saying. He leaned out of his cab and, with a twinkle that reflected Kate's mischievous mood, said tersely, "*Sakhar!*"

Kate stared at Olga for confirmation. "Are they really queuing for sugar? All those people!"

Olga shrugged, her expression sulky. "Is possible. Some temporary delay in delivery."

But the driver would not let her get away with excuses. "No sugar for a month," he told Kate in Russian. "Don't ask *me* where it vanishes!"

Kate judged it best not to ask Olga either. "Take no notice of this man," said the Russian girl sharply. "Let us go. I have errands for Dr Yasnov." Kate called a cheerful thank you to the driver and got out.

"If you have things to do for Dr Yasnov I can perfectly well —"

"No, no! I have been given the responsibility. Also, I am glad to practise my English."

Clearly she intended to stick like a leech. Good manners struggled with resentment in Kate's mind. Somehow she must escape, but without unpleasantness.

She racked her brain for a solution. The

pavements were thronged with people in holiday dress. At street-crossings, especially, the crowd made it hard to keep together. She determined to prepare the ground.

"If we should get separated," she said as casually as she could, "don't worry about me, I'll find a taxi —"

"We shall not be separated." Olga's tone was as positive as a political manifesto. "You will *not* miss me."

The band sounded much closer. Round the corner marched a procession of girls and boys in the crisp white uniforms and bright red neckerchiefs of the Young Pioneers. The sun flashed back from their shining instruments. Wide banners, inscribed with worthy slogans, swayed and flapped over their heads.

Olga paused on the kerb to explain. At school she herself had, of course, been a Young Pioneer, indeed a group leader. She had gone on to join the Young Communist League, the Komsomols. One day she would become a fully-fledged Party member.

"Aren't you now?" Kate's voice showed her surprise.

Olga took it amiss. "Oh, no! Membership is a great privilege. One must apply, one must study the teachings of Karl Marx and Lenin, one must show qualities of self-discipline." Her eyes became starry. "It will be a proud day when I receive my Party card."

She need not have bothered. Kate knew the shortcomings of Soviet society but she was equally well aware of its achievements. Olga need not spoil the morning with her lecturing and patriotic gush.

"How do we get to the beach?" Kate asked.

"First we must go to the Post Office. As we go, I shall point out the principal public buildings and monuments. The best shops, also."

"You're too kind," said Kate, poker-faced.

It was getting very hot. And the pavements very hard. She was not particularly interested in the best shops. She would have preferred to prowl round an open market or explore the side-streets where individual craftsmen plied their skills and where there might be tiny shops run as private enterprises instead of by the State.

She wondered if there was a Russian word for "junk-shop", but felt certain that Olga would not approve of such a place.

"Ah!" cried the Russian girl, suddenly. "Something is happening here!"

They were approaching one of those grim concrete buildings whose blankness was broken only by gigantic chunky sculptures of heroic miners or toiling peasants. It was just the sort of art that Olga admired and she was all set for a spate of explanation.

Kate was spared. Passers-by were clustering as a black, official-looking car glided to a halt. Policemen sprang forward, smart in their blue shirts and red-banded caps.

"Oh, you are lucky, Kate! Comrade Shulgin himself! You are seeing him on your very first morning!"

Three men had got out of the car and were crossing the pavement. The policemen's salutes, the eyes of the bystanders, the respectful murmurs of greeting were all directed at the first of them, a burly, barrel-chested man with a bushy moustache. He glanced round him rather grandly, acknowledging the reception. He was not bad-looking, thought Kate – he had a rough, rascally handsomeness. He was not one of those thin-lipped, dour-faced notables you usually saw on the news.

For a split second his eyes rested on her. And, as she instinctively dropped her own, her impression of him changed. Not a warm person, really, she decided. The eyes were chilly. Calculating. Probably ruthless. He made her shiver.

He mounted the steps and strode into the building.

"Who did you say that was?" She tried to sound casual and was vexed to find her voice shaky.

Olga's answer was ecstatic. "Anatoly Shulgin!"

"Is he someone important?"

"*Important?*" echoed Olga, horrified. She explained at length why Comrade Shulgin was so important, the posts he held, his popularity and influence throughout the region. Kate could not grasp all the elaborate jargon of Soviet councils and committees for this, that and the other, but she was left in no doubt – Shulgin was the big man here, a Party boss, and Olga regarded him with devout hero-worship.

"He stared straight at me," said Kate.

"It would be your English clothes. He misses nothing. He wants to encourage western tourists."

"He wouldn't encourage *me*." Kate was candid. "I didn't much like the way he looked at me."

This was quite the wrong thing to say. Olga bristled. I must try to be more tactful, Kate resolved. But, she thought with a stronger determination, I must give "Nanny" the slip.

They strolled on. Glancing across the street, Kate glimpsed enticing byways of the sort she loved to explore. But they would be no fun in Olga's company, even if she permitted such straying from her conducted tour. Kate grew more rebellious with every dreary statistic her guide poured out for the improvement of her mind.

They were passing a large store. "Look at those handbags!" cried Olga with enthusiasm. "They are new! You were criticizing the shortage of consumer goods in our shops. But have you such handbags in your London shops?"

"Yes," said Kate tartly, and was immediately thankful that her voice was lost in the blare of another approaching band. Behind it a seemingly endless column of Young Pioneers was marching down the street.

Olga was rapt in her admiration of the window-display. Kate saw her chance. It was unforgivable – afterwards she blushed at the recollection of her rudeness – but she had seen her chance and must not miss it.

Just as the head of the procession drew near she stepped off the kerb and dashed across the road in front of it. When she looked back, the people on the pavement she had just left were blotted from view by a line of tossing scarlet banners.

Even if Olga had seen her go, the law-abiding Russian girl would never break through the ranks of marching children. And, by the time they had gone, Kate would have vanished down one of those shadowy side-streets.

TWO

Remorse mingled with relief before Kate had gone more than a few yards down the side-turning.

If Olga had not seen her go, it could all be explained as an accident. Kate had been attracted by a shop on the other side of the street . . . they had been separated by the Pioneer parade . . . she had been unable to find Olga again.

A thin excuse? If Olga saw through it, too bad. At least she might take the hint that Kate was happier if left to her own devices. Kate was more worried about what her father would say if he heard of the incident. She had a feeling that the kindly Dr Yasnov would understand and forgive.

A glimpse of blue sea showed at the end of the street. She hurried towards it. Emerging upon the promenade she was dazzled by the glare. The heat struck her like the opening of an oven door. There were tufty little palms, acacias and oleanders lining the sea front, but the shade they cast at noon was minimal.

She saw at once why the Russians loved this Crimean coast. Most of the vast population lived much further north, where winter was harsh and long. Yalta, with its Mediterranean climate, must be a Mecca to them when the holiday season arrived.

She had better call the sanatorium at once, leave a reassuring message for Olga. Otherwise that over-conscientious young woman would get the blood hounds out to trace her. She found a public telephone, dropped a two-kopeck coin into the slot and dialled the number. The coin clinked as it fell. A defensive female voice said, "Allo?" She knew that Russians answering the phone did not identify themselves.

"Is that the Arkady Gaidar Sanatorium for Children?"

"Yes," admitted the voice. It became less suspicious, and eventually cordial, when Kate mentioned Dr Yasnov's name and explained that she had become separated from Olga.

"You want a car to be sent to collect you?"

"No, no, thank you very much. Just to leave a message for her. I shall get lunch in the town and take a taxi back."

"Very well. I will give her the message if she calls us. Or when she returns to her office."

"Thank you." Kate hung up, relieved. That disagreeable little matter was done with. She was never happy telling lies, but it was sometimes hard to avoid it.

There was still the risk, of course, of running into Olga. The sea front was an obvious place to look for her, but she could do nothing about that. She would just have to stick to her story.

As she strolled on, threading her way through the crowds of holiday-makers, her gaze was caught by what, for a few moments, seemed an incredible sight.

Rising above the fringe of trees were the masts and rigging of an old-time sailing ship. But clearly the vessel was not riding at anchor – the sea was some distance away, with a wide expanse of beach between. This vessel was right up against the promenade, indeed, it looked as though it were *on* the promenade, it towered so high above the treetops.

Noticing Kate's puzzled expression, a smiling woman said, "*Hispaniola!*" And when Kate replied in Russian, she was encouraged to explain. The ship was a full-scale replica of the famous schooner in *Treasure Island*. It had been built for a film production of that classic, and now it had been set up on the sea front as a bar and restaurant for foreign tourists using the luxurious Oreanda Hotel across the road.

"You may use it – you are English, yes? For a drink or a meal. For me, no," said the woman with a wistful shrug, and walked away.

As she drew nearer Kate could see the tourists at tables along the bulwarks and white-jacketed stewards moving to and fro with trays of drinks. But she felt no temptation to climb the gangway. No doubt everything would be of the very best, and priced accordingly. But she was not going to squander her allowance to sit among a crowd of foreign tourists. She could do that any day in London. She wanted to see the real Russia.

She went back to her original intention. She would explore the side-streets. And even as she made the decision she was spurred to instant action by the sight, some distance ahead, of a familiar figure. Even amid those crowds the stalwart Olga was unmistakable. She was coming this way at a purposeful pace, swinging her head from left to right, scanning the passers-by like a bird in quest of prey.

Kate stepped smartly round a corner, quickened her own speed almost to a run and, having whipped round two more corners, slowed to a walk again, feeling safe from discovery.

She paused for breath outside a little shop, the most interesting shop she had seen that morning. It was not exactly a junk-shop. There were valuable items mingled with odd pieces of old-fashioned china, carved wooden toys and second-hand skates, souvenirs from the Nazi war and samovars which must have been dispensing tea ages before the 1917 Revolution.

What leapt to her eye was a set of chess-men in time-yellowed bone; not great art but distinctively Russian. The head-dresses were of tsars and tsarinas, grand dukes and bishops of the Orthodox Church, every detail recalling bygone days. She checked swiftly. The set was complete, not a pawn missing.

Her father was a keen player. It would be ideal for his birthday and the perfect souvenir of their trip together.

She must hide her eagerness. Second-hand dealers were the same the world over. She stepped inside casually, idly fingering several objects before the bead curtains swished at the back of the shop. A plump, pleasant-looking woman, like a larger version of the painted wooden dolls on the counter, came through.

"American, yes?"

Kate was getting used to that mistake. "*Nyet,*

Anglichanka." Better show that she spoke Russian.

It paid off. The woman beamed. Many foreigners came. Very few knew the language.

Kate enjoyed the chat, but she did not forget her objective. Glancing idly round she pointed and said, "Is that a chess-set?"

"Yes, yes. Curious, isn't it? Carved from walrus tusks."

"Is it very expensive?"

"No. It's not of great antiquity. About 1900."

Kate's hopes rose. She might have enough Russian currency to buy it.

The woman lifted the White King and read the tiny label stuck on the base. "Two hundred roubles."

Kate's hopes fell. To her, compelled to change money at the official rate of only one rouble to the pound sterling, it was two hundred pounds!

"I am sorry," she said, "but it is more than I can afford."

The woman shook her head apologetically. "It is not possible to reduce the price."

The shop, she explained, was run on the *komissionny* system. People brought in their unwanted items, a sale price was agreed and she took only a fixed percentage of what the buyer paid, handing over the rest to the original owner. The chess-set would probably sell quickly, but if it did not she would ask the owner to consider marking it down. If Kate cared to enquire again in a month's time. . .

"I shall not be here," said Kate sadly, and took her leave.

She had gone only a few yards when a voice spoke behind her.

"American lady?" It was a low voice, soft and insinuating. A man's voice.

Instinctively she spun round. "*Nyet. Anglichanka.*" Then, vexed with herself for answering, she turned resolutely and stalked on. The street was empty. She heard his footsteps following. She braced herself. Would it be silly to break into a run? After all, it was not midnight but high noon.

The man spoke again, in a pleading wheedling tone. "You want roubles, lady? I change roubles. Very good rate. Best rate in town."

She was relieved. Just one of the black market currency touts. She'd met plenty in Moscow. He was not a mugger, anyhow.

"Is not good, is not fair," he was panting now at her elbow. "I give three roubles for one pound sterling. Not one for one!"

"No, thank you," she said firmly, not slackening her pace.

"Five roubles! Five roubles for English pound!"

It was terribly tempting. If he went on like this – and some touts, she had heard, would pay eight or ten roubles for a pound – by the time they reached the end of the street she might be able to buy the chess-set.

But it would be madly dangerous to accept. She knew what a serious offence it was to change foreign currency on the black market. She was not just afraid for herself, if caught. It would mean terrible embarrassment for her father. Perhaps mean the ruin of their whole visit.

"Seven?" offered the tout. His outstretched hand clutched a wad of rouble notes.

"Leave me alone, or I shall find a policeman. . ."

She would not have to look far. The street was no longer quite empty. Near the end, standing in the black shadow of an acacia, was a uniformed figure. How long had he been there, observing them?

The tout gave up. He turned away, streaked across the road and disappeared under an archway.

She walked on, flashing a grateful smile at the policeman whose timely appearance had saved her from further pestering. But the face under the peaked cap wore no answering look of friendliness.

A gloved hand shot out to bar her passage, and she stopped abruptly with a sudden unreasoning surge of alarm.

THREE

"Passport," demanded the policeman curtly.

In Moscow no one had ever demanded her passport. Kate had heard that everything was freer now. All that official bullying belonged to the bad old days.

"I'm so sorry, but I —"

"Passport!" Her Russian had not brought the usual responsive smile. The sallow features were full of suspicion.

"I haven't got it with me, I'm afraid."

"You are staying at the Oreanda? Or the Hotel Yalta?"

"No."

"But you are foreign? All foreign tourists —"

"I am not exactly a tourist."

"You will come with me. You will explain to my superior."

She had no choice. They set off, his boots clumping on the pavement beside her softly pattering trainers. She would have been thankful to turn a corner and come face to face with the forsaken Olga.

She did not. They walked for five minutes. Her wooden-faced escort ignored her protests. So much for the boasted new freedom, she thought bitterly. It did not seem to have penetrated to the south.

She was a little scared. Memories stirred of things overheard in childhood, headlined in newspapers, featured on TV. The Iron Curtain, spies, exiles, dissidents, forced labour camps, the midnight knock of the secret police.

Her father's first visit to Russia had been made in that time – the age of bugged rooms and tapped telephones, of mystifying obstructions and un-explained disappearances. It was all supposed to be changed now. It had seemed changed when they had got to Moscow. But, as a cynical American colleague had said to her father, "In Russia nothing ever really changes." Was that true?

Silly to be scared. The passport business was just a formality. She had been unlucky in running into a stupid policeman who would not listen to her explanation and insisted on dragging her off to the station.

Olga would have been really useful just now, even if she had crowed over Kate afterwards. She could still hear that prim voice, "For foreigners there can be all kinds of difficulties. Is better I go with you, I think."

Silly to be scared. Stalin, history's bogeyman, had been dead for ages. His hard-line successors were dead too. There was a new atmosphere in the Soviet Union. Surely?

This looked like the police station. Yes, they were going inside. Her escort muttered something to the man at reception. She was waved to a hard bench while her escort disappeared down a corri-dor. Another policeman lounged in the doorway. He was not obviously guarding her, but she felt sure that if she tried to leave she would be strongly discouraged.

She passed the time reading the notices plastered on the grey walls. She felt watchful eyes upon her. The man by the door was clearly intrigued because, though a young foreigner, she could read the announcements in their Cyrillic script.

Her own policeman returned. "The captain will see you." He took her down the passage, tapped on a door and stood aside for her to enter.

A fresh-faced young officer sat behind a desk. He looked rather grim but, when he spoke, his voice was pleasant enough. "Sit down, please. You speak Russian, I believe?" he said in that language.

"A little, sir."

"Excellent. We shall not require an interpreter." He drew a pad towards him and uncapped his pen.

Someone had entered the office behind her. She was conscious suddenly of a crude pervasive scent. The captain waved the newcomer to a seat. "I am sorry to trouble you. But it is as well to have a woman officer present."

"Just as well." A uniformed figure came into Kate's field of vision and slumped solidly into the offered chair. She too looked grim but in her case, Kate decided, it was probably natural. She wasn't so sure about the captain. Was he perhaps making an effort to be suitably grave?

The woman surveyed Kate critically. "She appears young. But that is nothing to go by."

The captain murmured a tactful warning. "She speaks Russian."

"Does she indeed?" Like Olga, this woman did not sound particularly pleased. Some people felt less secure when the language barrier was removed.

The man addressed himself to Kate. "Your name, please."

"Katharine Holford." She obligingly spelt it, remembering that, as there is no H in the Russian alphabet, her surname often caused a little hesitation.

He wrote it down. "British?"

"Yes."

"Your age?"

"Seventeen."

He allowed himself to smile. He was really rather good-looking, she decided. He said, "Permit me to congratulate you on your accent. Where did you learn?"

"At school. And some special coaching. I am going to read Russian at university. I have won a place at St Andrew's." She could not quite keep the pride out of her voice.

"You have no passport with you. But you told the militiaman that you were not staying at any of the tourist hotels here. Where are you staying?"

"At the Arkady Gaidar Sanatorium for Children."

He looked puzzled. "You cannot be a patient, you are too old. And you are too young to be a doctor or a nurse! What are you doing at the Gaidar?"

"I am the guest of Dr Yasnov."

The woman officer muttered something that

27

sounded like "That man", and indicated disapproval. The captain was more favourably
impressed and the only disapproval he showed
was conveyed in the irritated glance he shot at his
colleague, who sniffed and said no more.

"A most distinguished physician," he told Kate.
"You are privileged."

"I know. My father works in the same field –
children with all kinds of physical handicaps. He
and Dr Yasnov met at international conferences
and they became friends, being interested in the
same lines of research."

"Your father must also be a man of distinction
in your country?"

Kate smiled. "Well, I'm his daughter . . ." The
captain smiled back. "But obviously Dr Yasnov
thinks so. We've been at a congress in Moscow.
My father took me with him to interpret for him
and translate things. Dr Yasnov invited us here so
that they could continue their discussions and he
could show my father the work he was doing."

"Typical," murmured the woman sourly. She
was one of the old Soviet type, Kate guessed, who
believed that there should not be any over-
friendly contact with foreigners.

The captain continued his interrogation. "And
you arrived – when?"

"Only yesterday evening."

"Ah! That explains the passport."

"We know that we have to report our presence
to the local authorities within forty-eight hours.
But Dr Yasnov's office took our passports and
promised to do everything necessary. We should

have them back tomorrow."

"One moment. I will check." He lifted the telephone and spoke briefly. As he laid it down again he said, "All is in order. You will get your documents back tonight. You may need them," he added with disarming casualness, "if you wish to change money." He looked Kate straight in the eye. "The militiaman brought you in because, he said, you were behaving suspiciously."

"Suspiciously?" she echoed.

"You were in conversation with a well-known black market operator."

"Oh, that man? He was pestering me to exchange British money. I knew it was illegal."

The woman pounced. "You knew? So you cannot plead ignorance in your defence! We have established something."

"But I *did* nothing," Kate protested.

"You were seen coming out of a shop," said the captain gently. "Without your passport you could not have obtained roubles from a bank. If you had seen something you wanted to buy, might you not have been tempted?"

"I might well," she retorted hotly, "with the official exchange-rate so grossly unfair against us! But I'm not a complete fool. You have your rules. We have to keep to them." She was struggling to control her temper. On no account must she put their backs up. Officials, especially policemen, always had the last word.

"You can say that now," the woman sneered. "Naturally."

Kate thrust her hand into the pocket of her

denim jacket. She fumbled, pulled out her little wallet, slapped it on the desk. "Look. I have these roubles that I did not spend in Moscow. Ten, twenty, thirty, thirty-seven." She spread them out. "And here's the receipt they gave me when I changed them – at the official rate." She held out the printed slip, dated and stamped. Then she showed them her British currency, a couple of ten-pound notes.

"Thank you," said the captain quietly, "that is all perfectly in order."

She stuffed the notes back into her wallet and replaced it in her pocket. But the woman officer was not so easily satisfied.

"This proves nothing." She turned to her colleague. "When you sent for me I imagined that there might be some question of a body search for concealed currency. . ."

"There is not." His voice, when he chose, could be as stiff as hers. "And we have no right to make one. She has roubles which she has acquired in the proper manner. The British money is her own business. She has established her identity and the reason for her presence in Yalta. I am quite satisfied."

"Well, Captain," said the woman sulkily, "it is for you to say."

"Yes, it is for me to say."

He's pulling rank, thought Kate, with secret delight. How these two must hate each other!

The captain stood up and held out his hand. "You will accept our apologies, Miss Holford? A little misunderstanding – let us say an excess of zeal on the part of the militiaman? We hope your stay in our town will be enjoyable."

You may hope, she said to herself, but I don't know about your colleague.

She smiled amiably at them both and retired in good order.

FOUR

Outside in the sunshine Kate felt suddenly faint.

Nervous reaction? Nonsense, she told herself bracingly. Just no lunch. Breakfast so long ago.

She remembered that the sea front had been thick with street-vendors. She made her way back.

A man was selling freshly cooked *piroshkies*. They smelt marvellous. She bought one and sank her teeth rapturously through the hot pastry to the savoury meat filling. She went down on to the beach, munching.

Now, after the chill of the police station, she was glad of the hot sun beating down upon her. With some difficulty she found a vacant patch among the sprawling bodies and sat down. The big white pebbles were flat and smooth. Clean, too, although the Black Sea had really no tides. And the Russians seemed not to scatter litter.

Under her long eyelashes she stealthily surveyed her near neighbours. Not true that all Russian men were like enormous hairy bears. Not true that the women were like muscular puddings. Some of these girls. . . And as for their boy-friends!

She felt conspicuous, over-dressed amid all these bare bronzed figures. But it had felt fresh up at the sanatorium first thing this morning, and then Olga had swept her off so suddenly, giving her no time to change or get her bikini. Swimming would not have figured in Olga's programme for an instructive tour.

She licked her sticky fingers, and, more to cover her self-consciousness than because she wanted to write to Henry, pulled out her biro and the letter she had begun in the airport departure lounge in Moscow.

Henry was not strictly a boyfriend. He was merely a friendly boy, who sent her long screeds about his own doings which had to be answered occasionally, out of politeness.

Had to break off yesterday, she wrote, *because our flight was called. I'm in Yalta now. Fantastic place. More like the Mediterranean than Russia. I'm baking myself on a hot white (almost white-hot!) beach, surrounded by about a million Russians . . .*

Henry was not a person to whom she poured out her innermost feelings – which were, just now, that she was decidedly lonely. It did not do to confess things like that to Henry. He might jump to wrong conclusions.

As she searched her mind for the next harmless paragraph a shadow fell across her writing-pad. Someone had paused directly behind her – and had not moved on. She stiffened, pen in air, unable to frame the sentence.

She'd asked for it, of course, she told herself angrily – planting herself down here, so obviously alone. Be your age, she ordered herself sternly.

She could handle the situation – it wasn't the first time – but this didn't seem to be her day. Olga, the black-market tout, the busybody policeman . . . she seemed doomed to run into the wrong sort.

She would give a chilly answer. What was the Russian for "get lost" if this shadow made a pass at her? But the voice was a girl's, speaking in halting English.

"Excuse, please, pardon that I interrupt your writing. . ."

Kate twisted her head, squinting upwards into the glare. Considerately, the shadow dropped into a squatting position beside her. She was revealed as a slim figure in a bikini, much the same age as Kate, with curly dark hair tied back. She explained herself quickly.

"We are having a bet, my brother and I. Are you British or American? Or Scandinavian perhaps, or —"

"I'm English," said Kate good-humouredly.

"Fine! My brother insisted you were French."

"Why French?"

"Stepan thinks all truly elegant girls must be French!"

Kate was not displeased at the compliment, but she said, off handedly, "I don't *feel* very elegant, sitting here in jeans. I didn't know I'd get to the beach this morning."

The girl's eyes opened wide. "But they *are* elegant! We manufacture jeans ourselves now in the Soviet Union. But," she made a face, "they are not cut like these, they have not the style."

34

You'd better not let our Olga hear you say that, thought Kate, or she'll have you sent off to the Siberian salt-mines.

"I must not interrupt you longer," said the girl with obvious reluctance. "You did not mind I spoke to you like that?"

"Of course not!" Kate dropped into Russian, which brought a new sparkle into the stranger's brown eyes. "I'm very glad you did," Kate went on honestly. "I was feeling rather bored."

"Then perhaps you will come over and meet the others?"

Kate hesitated. "Shan't I be butting in?"

"Now there is no doubt that you are English!" The girl's laughter bubbled with delight. "This is the famous English reserve. It is unmistakable. But there is no one to introduce us! How terrible!" She held out her hand. "I am Marina Ushinskaya. Or, as we say, Marina Pavlovna."

Kate was familiar with the Russian custom. You used a person's father's name more often than her surname. Her own father's name, John, was "Ivan" in Russian, so, as she took Marina's hand, she could respond without hesitation, "I'm Katrina Ivanovna. At home my friends call me 'Kate'."

"Let us go, then."

Stepping carefully between the outstretched sunbathers they zigzagged up the beach towards two young men who were scrambling to their feet with broad grins of welcome. Marina's brother was tall, powerfully built, much fairer than she was, eyes blue, hair pale as straw. His friend was

35

small and swarthy, lively as a monkey and almost as hairy. Like many of the other sunbathers he wore a strip of white sticking-plaster on the bridge of his nose.

"Kostya's nose is very valuable," said Marina mockingly. "He guards it carefully from sunburn."

"And you are so vain of your classic Grecian features," Kostya retorted good-temperedly, "that you cannot bear to conceal them!" Though he mocked her it did not take long for Kate to realize how he really felt about her.

Marina had, in fact, the sort of nose you saw on beautiful nymphs and goddesses in museums. And it was, she always claimed, the genuine article. There had been Greek colonies all over the Crimea thousands of years ago. The very village in which she and Stepan had been born, on the hillside just above the town, had been built on ancient Greek foundations.

"Pottery fragments still turn up in the vineyards," she told Kate. "Some racial characteristics, in the same way, are traceable in the people. Some of that Greek blood lives on."

"Fascinating," said Kate.

"But quite unscientific," said Stepan. "There have been other Greeks much more recently. Refugees from Turkey in eighteen-something."

But no one wanted to argue about history. Kate was questioned keenly. What was life really like in the West?

"You are so lucky," said Stepan. "You can travel where you like. You have been to Paris?"

"Only for a week. With my school."

"But in London also you have splendid shops," said Marina wistfully.

Kostya was particularly interested in rock music. Had Kate heard of the famous Soviet groups, Autograph and Bravo Time Machine? She could not cope with his demand for up-to-date information about the leading British groups, the latest hits, the charts. He had a good collection of records.

"I have the new album of your Paul McCartney," he announced proudly. "New in our country, that is. It has just been released here. All the old rock songs of the Beatles! It is very difficult to get – there are not enough for all the fans who want them."

"So," said Stepan, changing the subject, "you are staying at the Gaidar Sanatorium?"

Kate explained how her father's friendship with Dr Yasnov had brought them here.

"And you too are to become a doctor?" Kostya inquired.

"No. I don't know what I shall do in the end." She told them that she was going to college in the autumn to study Russian language and literature. This delighted them, as a compliment to their country.

Stepan and Kostya had met at university. Stepan was to be a biologist and hoped eventually to get a post at the Institute of Viniculture here in his native Yalta. Kostya was absorbed in computers. He came from faraway Leningrad. For him, Yalta was just a wonderful place for a holiday.

"And I," said Marina, "work here in the film studios."

Kate exclaimed, much impressed, "How glamorous!"

Marina laughed. "No, no! I am not an actress. I work in the office." Even so, she admitted, there was some glamour in the work. She met famous directors, actors and actresses. There were certain advantages, little indirect contacts with the outside world. The actresses would come back from foreign festivals at places like Venice and Cannes. They would pass on discarded fashion magazines, give small presents of tights or toilet soap, nail varnish or lipstick, of a quality unobtainable in Soviet shops. Like Kostya with his rock music, Marina was remarkably well-informed on the subjects that most interested her, clothes, make-up and the British royal family.

While the girls chattered on about such matters, the men slipped away unnoticed, returning with four immense ice-creams. Kate accepted hers with delight. Their Russian ice-cream, she assured her new friends, was really something.

"*I* scream for ice-cream!" cried Kostya in English, and roared with laughter at his own pun.

Kate was now really enjoying herself. She was among her own age-group, making just the kind of contact she had hoped for.

"You must let us show you round while you are here," said Stepan.

"Tell us what you want to see," said Marina.

Kate had only one or two "musts". She must visit Chekhov's home, now a museum, where he had written two of the plays she most admired, *The Three Sisters* and *The Cherry Orchard*. And was it far to the house of the poet Pushkin?

Stepan reassured her. "No, Gurzuf is only about sixteen kilometres by the coast road."

There were other places she must see. The Tsar's former palace at Livadia, where Winston Churchill and President Roosevelt had held their famous Yalta conference with Stalin near the end of the Second World War. And the beautiful waterfall of Uchan-Su in its pinewoods. And the fantastical mansion of Alupka with its Moorish domes and minarets.

"But all these are the tourist sights," said Stepan impatiently. "We must show you other things – take you off the beaten track. You like walking? In the mountains? Excellent!"

At Marina's suggestion they agreed to meet for coffee at eleven o'clock the next morning. "Now we show you where to find a taxi," she said. "As we go, we will point out the café where we shall meet."

FIVE

In bed that night, the sea breeze fresh at the open window, the great trees murmuring from the moonlit grounds, Kate finished her letter to Henry.

> *I made a friend on the beach. I'm looking forward to meeting her tomorrow morning, and her —* Something checked her from writing brother. She substituted *friends* and continued, *It's interesting to hear their point of view, after all we've read in our own papers. There really is a new spirit here. They talk – constantly – of* "glasnost" *and* "perestroika".

She didn't need to translate those words. Everyone now knew that they were Russian for "openness" and "reconstruction", a clean break with the evil past. She smiled when she sealed the letter. Had she given Henry the impression that she was interested in these new friends simply because of their views on current affairs? Never mind . . .

Her father woke her next morning to say that their breakfast tray was waiting on his bedroom balcony. "With you in a moment," she said, and jumped out of bed. The sun was pouring into her room. Another wonderful day.

But a snag arose as she poured their tea. "Dr

Yasnov has asked me to his weekly staff conference," said Dr Holford briskly. "It's a good chance to meet everybody. Better bring your notebook."

She had not told him last night about Marina and the others. She could not tell him now. This, after all, was primarily what she had come for – to help him. She said, "OK, Dad. What time?"

He made a face. "Half-past eight, I'm afraid. They start work early here."

"Fine." That was a relief, anyhow. With luck they'd get through in time for her to keep her date with Marina.

Olga arrived punctually to collect them. She eyed Kate coldly and accepted her excuses for yesterday without comment.

Young patients were already appearing from the main building, the one-time mansion of the Grand Duke. Some of the children ran, some gamely hobbled using various aids, two were in wheelchairs. Olga firmly marched the Holfords down a shady avenue, away from the shouting and laughter.

"In summer," she explained, "Dr Yasnov likes to hold his staff conference in the open air. Is very pleasant. But – is far from telephone. For us, in the office, is not so good." Criticism tinged her voice.

Now the sea spread blue beyond the soaring cypresses. The land dropped sharply in rugged precipices. On a craggy spur a summer-house raised slender pillars like a miniature Greek temple, dazzling white against the cloudless sky.

41

A crowd of men and women were setting out cane chairs in a semicircle on the grass.

Dr Yasnov greeted them, smiling. "Thank you, Olga. I shan't need you now. You can get on with the letters."

"Very good, Comrade Director." She departed, acknowledging Dr Holford's thanks with a respectful inclination of the head, and pointedly ignoring his daughter.

On any other occasion Kate would have thought this toy temple, built at the whim of the Grand Duke, a delightful setting for the meeting. But at the back of her mind she was worrying too much about that other, very different kind of meeting. Would she get away in time? Would the young Russians wait for her if she was very late? She had no means of making contact with them if not. She did not know Marina's address. Kostya was staying in a students' holiday home, but she did not know which, and Yalta was full of such places.

Oh, it would be *too* bad if, having been lucky enough to make such friends on her first afternoon, she was to lose them again immediately.

Thank goodness, Dr Yasnov was businesslike. Always courteous to everyone, always relaxed and apparently unhurried, yet, she could see, with a splendid gift for keeping to the point and seeing that other speakers did. Questions were asked and answered, decisions amicably agreed. Kate scribbled busily when she heard anything likely to interest her father. But, when he was not looking, she took a stealthy peep at her watch.

She was agreeably surprised when suddenly, after a glance round the gathering, Dr Yasnov said, "No other points? Thank you," and rose to his feet.

Her relief was short-lived. Coffee was produced from the summer-house and, though a few people excused themselves and hurried away, her father was quickly surrounded by a cluster of surgeons and physicians wishing to be introduced. Some spoke English, and with some he could communicate in German or French as a common language. In other cases her services as interpreter were in great demand. And, if she was unoccupied for a few moments, someone was sure to buttonhole her with a word of personal welcome.

"A beautiful spot for a meeting," remarked a chubby-faced elderly woman, beaming at her with grandmotherly benevolence.

"Beautiful," Kate agreed. "Though I gather the office staff don't like the director being so far from his desk!"

"They can reach him if it is important," snorted the woman, who proved to be an eminent expert in physiotherapy. "The incessant telephone is a great time-waster. We can discuss our cases here without interruption. But there is another advantage about an outdoor meeting: it cannot be bugged."

"Bugged?" Kate stared.

"Oh, yes. There was too much of that, before.

Now, thank God, we can speak our minds freely."

Of course, thought Kate. This woman must have grown up in the terrible Stalin years. Her professional life would have been mostly under the dictators who succeeded him – what people now dared to call "the years of stagnation". Even more than young Marina and Stepan, she had cause to rejoice in the freer atmosphere of today.

She would have enjoyed a longer chat. But the digits on her watch were flicking inexorably to remind her of passing minutes.

The crowd had thinned to a tiny cluster. Her father, she saw, was safely under Dr Yasnov's wing, preparing to walk back with him to the sanatorium. He waved to her. "Thanks, Kate! Have a good day! You'll be all right?"

"Yes, Dad. Quite all right. Bye!"

She fled thankfully. She almost ran to the guest-block, dumped her notebook, and grabbed the beach-bag she had already packed.

She still might do it. If she'd had more warning she might have been able to book a taxi to run her down. Too late now. You couldn't tell what delays there might be, waiting for it to arrive. And she would most likely have to do it through Olga. No, she wasn't going to ask favours from *her*. Besides, she wouldn't put it past Olga to make deliberate difficulties – especially if she guessed why it was so urgent. Olga might take her revenge by sabotaging the whole thing.

She remembered there was a bus-stop outside the sanatorium gates. She hurried past the huge stable block, where once the Grand Duke had housed his scores of glossy horses, his fleet of coroneted carriages. Now it was all staff quarters and store rooms and an X-ray department – only the splendid black and gold clock remained, high on the pediment. And that clock was striking eleven.

The drive seemed endless. She had not covered it on foot before, had not realized its length, uncoiling like a snake with unnecessary sweeping curves to right and left. No doubt the Grand Duke – or more likely his Grand Duchess – had wanted it as long as possible so that the noble guests approaching their mansion would have time to admire the statuary and the unusual trees, collected from all parts of the world, and would get an exaggerated impression of the extent of the grounds. With the cheap labour of that period, what did it matter if the sinuous design added another quarter of a mile or so?

It took her nearly twenty minutes to reach the lodge-gates opening upon the public highway. She was sweating with the physical effort and anxiety. This really was maddening.

There was just an old, old man squatting by the bus-stop, rolling a cigarette. She greeted him. "When will the next bus come, Grandfather?"

He raised his faded eyes. "Soon."

Some minutes passed. "When is 'soon'?" She stretched out her bare arm, holding her wrist almost under his nose. But either he was blind or could not make anything of her digital watch, for he turned his head the other way, spat into the roadside dust, and said, "It will come when God sends it."

More minutes passed, but no bus. It looked as though the Almighty did not accord a high priority to Yalta's local bus service. She was close to despair when the sanatorium truck came rattling through the gates and swung round to a shuddering halt beside her. It was Sergei, the same driver as yesterday. Gasping her gratitude, she leapt up beside him. The old man had not stirred. Either he was not waiting for the bus at all, or he felt unequal to such a strenuous scramble. Sergei drove off.

Kate explained her urgency. "What café?" he asked. She felt a fool – she had not noted the name, only its appearance and location. She knew she could find it. "I cannot drive along the sea front, but I can drop you very near. Have no fear – your friends will wait for you. Anyone would wait for you!" he ended gallantly.

To be on the safe side, however, he accelerated violently. Perhaps "to be on the safe side" was not the most appropriate phrasing, thought Kate wryly as she clung nervously to her seat. Sergei drove with the high-spirited abandon of a Cossack galloping headlong over the steppe. She closed her eyes at the most terrifying of the bends.

It was a few minutes after twelve when she arrived breathless at the café and surveyed the tables dotted about under the trees. There would have been no difficulty in identifying Stepan. But, though there were two or three handsome and hefty young fellows with similar fair colouring, there was no sign of Stepan or his sister or the lively Kostya.

Sergei had been too optimistic. They had not waited. Or – a sudden, even more depressing, explanation occurred to her – had they changed their minds after leaving her yesterday, and decided not to keep the appointment?

She recalled some of her father's earlier Russian experiences during the years of suspicion when people were frightened of personal contacts with visiting foreigners. Even the friendliest Russians had never invited him into their homes. Sometimes, having promised to meet him in a public place, they had unaccountably failed to turn up.

All that was past history now. Or was it? Stepan and his sister didn't look the sort to get cold feet – after all, Marina had spoken to *her* first – but had they nervous parents, who had begged them not to take chances? Parents worried absurdly about the simplest things.

Disappointed, thoroughly deflated after all the effort she had made, she turned and walked aimlessly along the sea front. She was now in the smartest area of the town, with the best shops and restaurants, catering largely for foreign tourists. In five minutes she caught snatches of as many different languages.

In one shop doorway an American woman was holding up a pair of ornate earrings and firing questions at the young saleswoman. The Russian girl, puzzled but eager to oblige, tried French and German but without avail.

"Can I help?" Kate murmured.

The American spun round. She was blonde, good-looking, but perhaps, thought Kate, unwise to wear trousers.

"Say, that would be real kind! These folk don't seem to understand any language but their own."

Kate was able to hide her smile by turning quickly to the saleswoman and offering to interpret. The girl's gratitude was obvious. "I speak only a few words of English," she admitted.

"The lady wants to know how old the earrings are."

"I think they are of the late nineteenth century. They are not costly, but if one admires the work of that period they have their charm."

Kate translated this. "I'm just crazy about earrings," confessed the American. "I've a collection back home you wouldn't believe! I can't resist 'em. Late nineteenth century, she says? Would you call that Tsarist, now?"

"Certainly. Time of the last emperor, Nicholas II."

"My, you know all about it, I guess! That'd be the poor man the Bolsheviks murdered in the Revolution?"

"Well, yes, actually. But," Kate felt slightly embarrassed, "it might be a bit tactless to talk about that just now."

"That's OK with me. It's the price of the earrings I want to know."

To Kate's relief the woman made no attempt to haggle about the price when it was worked out in its dollar equivalent. She snapped open her handbag and produced a wad of rouble notes.

As soon as the transaction was completed Kate began to make her farewells, but the American detained her with a hand so heavily beringed that Kate concluded she must collect them too.

"I guess this calls for a little drink, honey. I know I could use one myself."

"Oh no, really —"

But Pearl Hathaway, as she now introduced herself, was not to be denied. She was, as Kate had already suspected, a person of formidable character.

"We'll have it on board the yacht," she announced. "It's tied up just over there." Her plump hand indicated the marina close by.

This made the idea more attractive. Kate loved new experiences. She had never been on board a sea-going yacht and she accepted without more ado. She had missed her friends. The day now stretched blank before her.

They threaded their way through the crowds on the quay. Walking behind Mrs Hathaway, Kate noticed how many admiring glances they attracted – and she was well aware that it was the American woman who drew them. Pearl Hathaway made an imposing figure. Though her yachting outfit did not permit high heels, she had a magnificent walk, with a roll of the hips that suggested a model's training. Indeed – as Kate was to learn within the next half-hour – she had begun as a model. She had been beauty queen of her own state. But of what state, and in which year she had won the title, Mrs Hathaway never disclosed.

The marina was full of craft. The *Meltemi* was

a graceful but not luxurious-looking vessel. Though the Soviet flag fluttered, out of courtesy, above the wheelhouse, it was the Turkish ensign at the stern that proclaimed her actual nationality.

"Here we are," said Mrs Hathaway, stepping on to the little boarding platform and holding out a welcoming hand. Boarding was easy. With the Black Sea having no tide, craft could be moored without regard for rise and fall in the water-level.

An almost vertical little ladder led up to the deck. Mrs Hathaway mounted it with remarkable agility. She's certainly fit, thought Kate, as the well-tailored haunches rose above her and vanished beyond the rail. She followed and, a few steps forward past the wheelhouse, found herself in the cool shadow of an awning which covered the deck from side to side.

A Turkish lad was arranging wicker chairs. There was a chatter of voices from below. "I guess Mike and the others are downstairs," said Mrs Hathaway, who clearly had no use for correct nautical terms. "C'm on, honey."

Kate followed her down a companionway into the saloon, where about a dozen men and women were being offered drinks by a smiling podgy little man. A shining halo of wiry silver hair rose in a fringe around temples that were copper-brown from sea and sun.

"Welcome aboard!" He broke off to greet Kate. Mrs Hathaway made the introductions. He was Michael Flann. "Kate's British," she added.

"No need to tell me! Glad to know you, Kate. Fine. We just needed a touch of youth and beauty." He grinned wickedly round the company, all middle-aged, and they laughed politely. She flushed. He meant no harm. He was just. . . She had not quite decided just what he was when he was demanding, "What'll you drink, Kate?"

She hesitated. Mrs Hathaway – "Pearl", as she insisted on Kate's calling her – came promptly to her aid. "None of your tricks, Mike," she said with a warning edge to her voice, "none of your famous 'specials'. Just something long and cool, eh, Kate?"

"That would be lovely. Thanks."

Flann mixed her drink and dropped ice into it under Pearl's watchful eye. Whatever it was, it cheered Kate up considerably after the earlier disappointment of the morning.

This is an odd sort of party, she thought as she sipped her drink and listened to the chatter round her. None of the other guests seemed to be sailing in the yacht. It would surely hold six or eight in comfort and most people would have filled it with friends for the trip. But Mike and Pearl clearly had the vessel to themselves, except for the three Turkish crewmen who padded silently to and fro, refilling glasses and offering little dishes of fresh anchovies and other Black Sea delicacies.

Kate's fellow guests all appeared to be Americans, tourists staying at the expensive Oreanda. They knew each other only slightly, their host and hostess hardly at all. From their talk Kate guessed that they had been picked up almost as casually as she had herself.

No doubt their hosts had been eager for social

life after days of solitary cruising. Kate could believe that easily of Pearl. She was hungrily questioning her guests about affairs "back home", the fashions and gossip, the latest Broadway shows.

Mike Flann was very different.

Clearly he loved an audience. *He* was not seeking information – only a chance to impart it. He was an enthusiast, a fanatic almost, an eccentric certainly. There was a framed chart hanging in the saloon. He stood by it, holding forth with a passionate eloquence.

"Ye ask me why I come to the Black Sea? Because it's fascinatin'! It's the sea o' myth and legend."

"You can tell Mike's Irish," Pearl murmured in Kate's ear.

"Irish?"

"Irish-American – one of the New York Irish." Pearl laughed softly. "We have a joke, folks say all the New York cops are Irish. But I don't see Mike as a cop, not his style exactly." Was it imagination, Kate wondered, or was there a certain significance in her tone? As Pearl moved on to other guests, she stayed to listen to this pot-bellied little man with the shock of wild silvery hair.

"Everyone makes for the Isles o' Greece," he cried scornfully, "but see here, will ya?" He tapped the chart. "Where did Jason go lookin' for the Golden Fleece? Kolkhida, it says here! That's the old-time Colchis. Where the Argonauts sailed in the Argo. Right here was where Medea lived,

Medea the witch. And see the Caucasus mountains behind? Where Prometheus was chained to the rock while the eagle pecked out his liver!"

The gruesome legend provoked a ripple of horror and amusement from his listeners. He swept his hand triumphantly across the chart.

"It's like that everywhere, hereabouts – the old Greeks came to the Crimea too. 'Tauris', they called this area. Euripides called one of his plays *Iphigenia in Tauris*." He stabbed at the place with his finger. "See here? Balaklava? They found the ruins of Iphigenia's temple right here!"

His enthusiasm was infectious. He must be quite self-educated, Kate judged. Got it all from books. He mispronounced names, saying "*Meed*ea" and "Iph*igeen*ia" as if he'd never heard them spoken. She respected people who hadn't been to college but read books and found out things for themselves. Actually there wasn't a book in sight, but no doubt they'd been tidied away.

"It's all legend surely, Mr Flann?" suggested one of the men. "Not much solid evidence —"

Their host turned on him fiercely. "There's the whole atmosphere to respond to! But plenty o' history too." He pointed. "The Romans came here. That's why it's still called Romania. The frontier o' their empire! This was where their great poet Ovid was sent for exile . . ." He was off again. No one else ventured to interrupt the flow.

Kate wondered if Pearl shared his interests. It must be boring for her with no other company on board. She must be very devoted to her Mike. All the same, there was something hard to explain.

The whole set-up seemed distinctly odd.

Suddenly Kate became aware of a steady vibration under her feet. She glanced through the porthole. She was startled to see that the dazzling white harbour buildings were swinging away. The yacht was heading purposefully towards the open sea.

SIX

Kate did not like to interrupt Flann. She went across to her hostess.

"Excuse me, Mrs Hathaway."

"Pearl, please, honey!"

"Where are we going? I didn't realize —"

"No cause for alarm. Did you think you were being shanghaied or something?"

The other women cackled. Inwardly furious, Kate struggled to sound casual. "It's only about getting back . . ."

"We'll not be late. Mike just wants to show off this boat of his. Give you all a fresh view of the coast from out yonder."

"That'll be real nice," someone said. "We'd sure all appreciate that."

There was a general move up to the deck. Flann showed them the wheelhouse, introducing Yusuf who was at the helm, negotiating the harbour-mouth and the busy traffic of small craft moving in and out. Kate caught snatches of the technical chatter. Cruising speed, 10 or 12 knots . . . 11 tons displacement . . . 9 metres overall . . . Italian-built, at Genoa . . . can't beat the Italian designers if you want a real elegant job . . .

Reassured that they were only going for a quick trip round the bay, she leant on the rails and took in the ever-widening panorama. The town had become a decorative pattern of green and white blotches, mingling the rich foliage with the buildings. Behind, hung a dove-grey frieze of crinkled precipices.

Flann was pointing out Ayu-Dag, or "Bear Mountain". It was indeed shaped like a gigantic bear, crouched over the sea.

"You gotta admit this is *the* most fantastic coast! Wish we'd more time, I'd just love you folks to see it all. Swallow's Nest, on the cliffs at Ay-Todor, an' At-Bas, the 'Horse's Head', an' Koshka – that's 'Cat Mountain' – an' the Devil's Staircase, Chortova Lestnitsa." He reeled off the names. He knew every landmark on these coasts. He'd been coming to the Black Sea for several years.

Yalta had slipped from view behind them. Kate wondered uneasily when they would start to turn back. It was a real bonus, this panoramic view from the sea – she realized now how high the mountains were, towering up beyond the coastal strip – but she must not be late back at the sanatorium.

At last the yacht began to slacken speed. Then it stopped, bobbing gently on the waves. An official-looking launch was coming out as if to intercept them.

"Coastguards, maybe," somebody remarked.

"Cops, I guess," suggested another guest knowledgeably.

Oh, not *again*, thought Kate. She was not seriously dismayed, but it would be a strange coincidence if she found herself involved with the police and delayed for a second time.

Flann's manner changed abruptly. The eccentric

enthusiast became instantly alert. "Excuse me, folks." He moved aft, pausing to touch Pearl's arm in passing. Kate heard him murmur, "Keep things goin', honey. I gotta —" He hurried past the wheelhouse and vanished down the ladder to the boarding platform.

Kate craned over the rail as the launch came chugging alongside. She caught a glimpse of a thickset figure swinging himself nimbly aboard. A second man followed. The launch veered away again, tracing a frothy curve towards the shore.

"Bit of bureaucracy," snorted a lady at Kate's elbow. "They're still just *so* suspicious of foreigners, these Soviets."

To Kate's ear, however, the voices sounded cordial enough. As Flann's silver halo of hair bobbed into view again, leading the newcomers up to the deck, he appeared to be entirely at ease.

He was introducing the nearest of his guests. "This is Professor Ruddock – and I'd like you to meet Mrs Gallimore, a noted expert in the field of . . ." Kate never heard in what field Mrs Gallimore was notable. She edged back, modestly effacing herself. Although Flann was relaxed she imagined that a faint note of deference had crept into his tone, as though he wished to impress the strangers with the importance of his guests. He was striving, she thought amusedly, to make the most of his hastily collected party.

The first Russian was answering in English. A careful, heavy English, with a distinctly transatlantic ring. "You enjoy yourselves in our town? We are most eager to develop the tourism —"

Flann broke in, offering him a choice of whiskies. "Bourbon, please! I acquired a taste for it when I was a young man, serving with our trade delegation in New York." That brought a chorus of questions from the New Yorkers present.

Kate edged further into the background, leant on the rail and contemplated the mountains that rose steeply from the coast road, their flanks lined with vine-terraces, with shaggy woodlands or bare rock above. She had no taste for humdrum party chitchat. This official, whoever he was, would not be interested in meeting an obscure young student.

Flann, however, had his eye on her and was not leaving her out. She heard his voice suddenly, just behind her. "And this young lady is Kate Holford, from England. Her father's the distinguished physician, Dr Holford. They're visiting with your famous Dr Yasnov."

Kate turned. She found herself face to face with the barrel-chested, bushy-moustached celebrity she had seen getting out of his car yesterday. Olga's hero. The local party tycoon.

With automatic politeness she put out her hand and it vanished into the strong, bear-like paw. Again, the calculating eyes under the thick eyebrows weighed her up and chilled her. The deep voice said, haltingly, "We are especially glad when our famous health resort attracts the notice of eminent medical men from abroad. I trust your father will pass an interesting time here."

"Thank you." For once she did not reveal her knowledge of Russian. It might seem rude when he was obviously taking such pains to speak her own language. "I will tell him what you say, Mr Shulgin."

He looked startled, but recovered himself immediately.

"Please do, my dear young lady, please do," he answered rather grandly, and moved on with Flann to greet another guest. The second Russian followed, a silent smiling shadow. Kate could not recall having seen him before.

It was her use of his name that had startled Shulgin. She realized why. Flann had not spoken it. And, as she became involved again in conversation with the tourists, she found that it had not been an accidental omission. Everyone was quietly speculating about the identity of this Russian. Flann had not named or explained him to anyone. That must have been deliberate for some reason, Kate concluded. At least it accounted for Shulgin's reaction when she answered him.

He was still completing his circuit of the deck, making himself agreeable, laughing, complimenting the ladies, holding out his glass to be refilled. Again, Kate saw Flann lay a discreet hand on Pearl's arm and caught his murmured instruction, "Take care o' this other guy, Shabelsky."

"Sure. Does he understand English?"

"Not much, I guess. Can't be sure. But he understands whiskey!"

"OK, Mike."

"I *gotta* have five minutes alone with Shulgin."

Flann turned away. Very soon he disappeared below with his Russian guest.

There really *was* something mysterious about this party, thought Kate. Why had she, of all people, been invited to it on the spur of the moment? Why, for that matter, these other guests, all like herself chance acquaintances? Why was the party taking place anyhow?

And then there was this creepy character, Shulgin. . .

Flann obviously knew him. Nothing remarkable about that, if the yacht paid frequent calls at Yalta. Shulgin's appearance had not taken him by surprise. Clearly the two men had something private to discuss. Private? Or secret?

Another idea occurred to her. Was the party hurriedly put on *because* of Shulgin's visit? Not because he really wanted to meet foreign tourists, but as a cover for his presence on board? Perhaps even a highly-placed official like Shulgin had to go carefully and not seem too friendly with foreigners from the West. To meet Flann at a party was harmless. A private conversation, like the one now taking place in the saloon, was another matter. If Shulgin had jealous enemies it could be made to look suspicious, and used against him.

That was where Pearl came in. She had been told to take care of the second Russian, Shabelsky. Ply him with whiskey. Make sure he didn't notice that Shulgin had vanished from the scene.

And Pearl had tumbled at once to what was required of her. Kate guessed it was not the first time she had been useful in this way. It had been quite interesting to watch, from the shadows under the awning, the practised skill with which the charming Mrs Hathaway had sailed into action.

The minutes passed slowly. The calm sea slapped gently at the vessel's sides. Kate drifted back into the party. She did not want to seem unsociable. The tourists were friendly, she answered their questions, secretly prayed that the yacht would soon get under way again. Thank goodness, the launch was coming back. She turned to the rail and craned over. One of the Turks was down there on the boarding platform, boathook ready.

Shulgin and Flann came up the companionway from the saloon. She caught their low-voiced exchange.

"Usual arrangements then?" murmured the American.

The deep-throated answer came from the Russian, "Agreed. The usual arrangements."

The launch was alongside. There was a little trouble, and some shocked laughter, over getting Mr Shabelsky down the steep ladder and back into the launch. His thanks and farewells were confused, but no one was left in any doubt that he had thoroughly enjoyed his visit to the yacht. How much he would remember of it in detail – especially his colleague's disappearance below – was less certain.

The launch sped away shorewards. The *Meltemi*'s engines throbbed into life. The yacht got under way, described a wide curve to starboard and headed back at speed for the harbour.

It looked very much as if the party was over.

Pearl kept up her lively conversation with the guests, but Flann, when he returned to the deck, seemed to have lost interest.

Kate ventured a question on the ancient Greek associations of Yalta, but her host's mind was clearly elsewhere. That imp of mischief which never deserted her for long prompted her to persist. She followed her question with one or two other apparently simple queries.

Twice he fenced, once he was forced to confess complete ignorance on some elementary general point. "I have to tell you I'm no college professor," he protested defensively. "This is my hobby. I don't know all the answers. I just go on niggling away, trying to figure them out." She felt slightly ashamed of herself. His modesty had become disarming.

Now the land, the high mountainous background, loomed ever taller beyond the *Meltemi*'s bow. The beaches stretched to right and left of the harbour-approaches, the water was dotted with the heads of swimmers. If the morning had gone right, thought Kate, she might have been one of them.

Perhaps her friends of yesterday were somewhere among them even now, but the chances of spotting them, among so many hundreds, were minimal. Would she ever see them again, she wondered sadly?

Five minutes later, as Yusuf skilfully steered the yacht through the harbour entrance, she did. They were not dots on the tremulous water but full-length figures standing on the quay –

unmistakably Marina, Stepan and Kostya, chatting to another man.

She waved. They must have seen her at that short distance, but they gave no sign of recognition. She did not like to shout, but she waved frantically. There was no answering wave. Marina and Kostya were turning in the opposite direction.

The yacht slid into her berth and was made fast. Kate thanked her hosts hurriedly, gabbled a few civil words to her fellow guests as they streamed off, and, as the others all strolled away towards their hotel, raced to the spot where her friends had been.

Had been. For there was no sign of them now. Friends? Could she still think of them as friends? She felt sure they had seen her. With a desolate feeling she turned and trudged back into the town. She was too proud to scour the sea front for them. There was nothing to do now but find the bus-station.

SEVEN

Kate had just finished typing out her notes of the morning's meeting when her father tapped on her bedroom door and poked his head in.

"We're invited to a meal with the Yasnovs tonight. Could you put on something a bit special?"

"Sure!"

"It's only ourselves. Not to worry unduly."

Kate had packed for this trip with some forethought. Formal clothes for conference functions in Moscow, casuals for sightseeing and the beach. Playing for safety, she had brought a simple ivory-white dress – "suited to your age," Mum had said – but not too demure. Rather stylish, in fact. It should do for this evening.

Prompt on the hour they walked across to the main building, which looked more like a stately home than a sanatorium. They mounted the curving marble steps and passed through the imposing doors. Even the Revolution and the conversion of the Grand Duke's home had not banished the original atmosphere of elegance and splendour. Under an immensely lofty, painted ceiling, they followed a white-overalled woman up a sweep of bronze-railed stairs and down a wide corridor to the Director's private quarters.

"Wow," Kate whispered.

Even now the tall white doors with their gilded fittings seemed to call for footmen in livery.

She had long ago realized that modern Russia

was rather different from what some of her school-friends pictured – a world of drab compulsory equality, expressed in overcrowding and shortages. That Russia certainly existed. But she knew, through her father, that some people enjoyed a higher standard of living if they were doing outstanding work of value to the community. Still, she had not expected even a man of Dr Yasnov's eminence to live in such a magnificent setting.

Inside, the Yasnovs' suite was not conspicuously luxurious. The rooms were naturally large and well proportioned, giving them much more living space than the average Russian couple could hope for. But the original furniture had long since disappeared, looted or wrecked in the early frenzy of the Bolshevik triumph. It had been replaced by massive, old-fashioned, rather shabby pieces. The litter of books and papers at once reminded Kate of home.

Madame Yasnova welcomed them with impulsive warmth. She spoke better English than her husband, so that there was no language problem for Dr Holford. She was surprisingly young – tall, graceful, really beautiful. How, Kate wondered, had she come to marry a little goblin like the Director, with his frog-like smile, gleaming bald head and upstanding ears?

Clearly, though, she was devoted to him. And determined that he should relax after his long working day. Before they were called to the table he had already embarked on a scientific discussion with his British colleague.

"We were speaking of side-effects this afternoon – especially from the cytotoxic drugs —"

"You may have been," she cut in firmly, "but, my dear, you will not speak of them tonight."

"But Dr Holford and I have so much —"

"There will be tomorrow." She wagged a stern finger, but laughed as she did so. "Tonight – what is your English expression, Dr Holford? – we shall not 'talk shop'. If I hear one word about bone-marrow transplants, or congenital abnormalities, or trauma-related incidents . . ."

Another white-overalled woman set bowls of soup in front of them. Kate was ready for it. She had missed a proper midday meal; she had had nothing but those insubstantial if delicious nibbles on the yacht. And Dr Yasnov, now very much on his best behaviour, was asking her politely if she had passed an interesting day.

"Very, thank you."

"Tell us," commanded Madame Yasnova, "all you have done."

Kate briefly described her encounter with Pearl Hathaway and her trip in the *Meltemi*.

Madame Yasnova pounced on the mention of Mr Flann. "I have heard of this mysterious American."

"Oh – *is* he mysterious?"

"He aroused some suspicion when he first appeared in these parts," Dr Yasnov explained. "It was the time of the Cold War. Any American in a private yacht, who might take photographs of the coastline, or even soundings in the water . . ."

"Your people thought he might be a spy?" said Dr Holford.

The director shrugged. "Our government then was paranoid about American intelligence. And I believe," he added, with his sly goblin grin, "the West had a certain obsession about Soviet agents?"

"From what Kate tells us," said his wife, "Mr Flann's obsession is much more with old myths and legends."

"He seems to be on good enough terms now with the authorities," said Kate. She began to tell them of Shulgin's sudden appearance at the party.

Mention of the Communist official produced a powerful reaction.

"That man will go anywhere for a drop of American whiskey," said Madame Yasnova acidly.

"Careful, my love." Her husband glanced towards the open door. The woman had cleared their soup-bowls but could be heard not far away.

"I thought we had finished nowadays with this need to whisper in corners!"

"I hope so. But it is still better to be careful when mentioning certain names. The gentleman in question has still many loyal admirers."

"Very well," said Madame Yasnova reluctantly, "I will be more discreet." As the woman returned with the next course she turned to Kate and lapsed into Russian, "Explain to your father, please, what a high regard we all have for this Comrade Shulgin you were fortunate enough to meet." When the woman had served them and gone out, she gave Kate a twinkling smile and reverted to English. "When I was a child I had great ambitions to become an actress."

There was no further mention of the important Party member, but the incident lingered in Kate's mind as significant – and somewhat sinister. In spite of all the changes in Soviet life some of the old fears evidently survived. Freedom of speech had still some way to go. It might be dangerous to criticize local leaders. Even the Yasnovs could be at risk if their remarks were reported.

"Let us take a stroll," suggested their hostess when the meal came to an end. "We shall catch the last of the sunset over the sea."

The sky was still brilliant over the treetops. The grounds were almost deserted, the young patients by now in bed. The volley-ball pitch stretched empty, the slides and climbing frames stood silhouetted, black and geometrical. Only a few of the staff stood chatting or flitted from one building across to another.

Kate recognized the shadowy figure of Olga. She wished the Director and his wife a respectful, almost unctuous, good-night. It was as well, thought Kate, that she had not heard their remarks about her hero Shulgin.

The evening air was fragrant with roses, but when they moved away from the formal gardens into the park-like area with massive trees they encountered a new scent.

"It is the acacias," said Madame Yasnova. "Yalta is famous for them."

One Grand Duke had planted rare trees

collected from all over the world – California and New Zealand, Asia Minor and Japan. There were spiky little palms and gargantuan masses of hydrangea. A Chinese Tree of Heaven sent its long branching arms thrusting to the crimson sky.

The Grand Duke had dotted the grounds with statues, mostly nineteenth-century copies of Greek or Roman or Italian Renaissance originals, although here and there stood older examples, battered and fragmentary but genuine. The Tsarist aristocrat had not been particular.

"If something *looked* ancient," said Dr Yasnov with a chuckle, "he bought it and fitted it in somewhere."

There were grottoes, too, their walls encrusted with everything from sea shells and oolites to scraps of pottery and jagged bits of marble reliefs.

A cypress avenue brought them to an ornamental pool, its water like blood, reflecting the red sky.

"Notice," said Dr Yasnov. "He had it dug out to the exact outline of the Black Sea. This bit that juts out, that we are standing on, this peninsula – it is the Crimea." It was just big enough to take the four of them. "This is now where the children swim," he said. They strolled on to another large pool, kidney-shaped. "This is the Caspian Sea. It is more shallow. Here we sail our model boats." Further on they came to a third, much smaller pool. This was the "Aral Sea", a paddling place for toddlers. "We are much indebted to the Grand Duke and his fancies," said Dr Yasnov.

"Don't the children ever get down to the real sea?"

"Certainly. We use a special section of the beach in Yalta."

The grounds ran to the cliff edge, with a strong fence for safety. There *was* a way straight down to the water, he said, but it was too steep and rough for handicapped children, and it led only to a cove where the rocks and deep water made it unsuitable for them.

"The Grand Duke and his guests bathed there. He had some steps made – it is still known as the Grand Duke's Staircase. Some of the staff have used the place occasionally – but if you should be tempted to swim there yourself I would advise you not to go alone."

"I won't," Kate promised.

"She's quite a strong swimmer," said her father, "but she wouldn't take silly risks."

"This is the beginning of the path." Yasnov pointed to it, a thin pale ribbon running down to the left. "This old stone marks the turning." It was set in a bank of earth, a smooth wedge-shaped slab, pierced by a large round hole at its narrower end.

They walked on. They came to a craggy spur from which they could best survey the dying glory of the sunset. Far below them the sea lay satin-smooth, stretching away to the invisible coast of Asia. They sat down for a few minutes. The rocks were still warm from the day's heat.

"I will take this chance, while we are alone and can speak quite freely," said Madame Yasnova. "I must explain why we had to cut short what we were saying at dinner about our famous Comrade

70

Shulgin. He has certainly a taste for western luxuries."

"He seems to have been to New York," said Kate.

"Yes. Unfortunately – for him – he was expelled from America."

"That is only gossip," protested Dr Yasnov. "There was some trouble certainly. He was recalled."

"Anyhow," said his wife firmly, "he has never been sent abroad again. You may draw your own conclusions."

"He seems to be a very important figure here," said Kate.

"He has made himself so! By fair means or foul. He has worked his way up the Party ladder. He knows how to manipulate the machine. He promotes his friends and eliminates his enemies. That was how it was done in Stalin's day – and long afterwards. He is a survival from that period."

"He is certainly a survivor," said Dr Yasnov with a dry chuckle. "Trust Shulgin! He is of the type that always survives. Like a virus! Science finds a drug to beat the virus, and the virus develops an immunity, appears as a new strain – and all the time the scientist is running behind, trying to catch up!"

"He makes a joke of it," said Madame Yasnova, speaking, as Kate sensed, with immense feeling. "But once this monster tried to destroy *him* – my husband!"

"Lisa!"

"It is true. So I will say it. We want our guests to understand our country, know the bad as well as the good. My husband has never applied to join the Party. He has always valued too much his freedom of thought as a scientist, his integrity." There was fierce pride in her voice. "In the early years it was a terrible handicap. For in medicine, as in other careers, the key positions went always to dependable Party members. It was almost unknown for the directorship of an institution like this to be awarded to a non-Communist. Alexei won it on merit – on brilliance – indeed there was no other candidate to touch him —"

"Really, Lisa," pleaded her embarrassed husband, but he could not silence her.

"Only this odious Shulgin tried to block the appointment. He wanted it for one of his yesmen. So he pulled strings, he stirred up prejudices, he mounted a campaign of slander. But he failed."

"This is ancient history! I beg you, Lisa —"

"I have said my say. But Kate and her father must realize that things have not always been easy."

Dr Yasnov was trying to smooth things over. "Many things have been wrong in the past. Much inefficiency, much corruption."

"Rackets – as Shulgin must have learned to call them when he was in America! He has a finger in all of them."

"But now we are promised sweeping reforms. Already, all over the country, corrupt officials are being exposed and dismissed —"

"But not here!" interrupted his wife. "Not Shulgin. He is too clever. He protects his henchmen so skilfully, he persuades the people that he is their best possible leader. You say yourself, Alexei, he is a survivor. And I tell you, so long as he remains, he is a danger. He has never forgiven *you*."

"I didn't like him," said Kate. "He gave me the shivers. I was surprised that Mr Flann welcomed him so warmly."

"Ah, that is something I will not speculate upon," said Madame Yasnova darkly.

The Director seized this chance to change the subject. "Let us not spoil this beautiful evening. At least Shulgin cannot control the sunset."

"Thank God!" His wife laughed, her good humour returning. "I am sorry, my friends. Let us talk of more pleasant subjects."

They turned back through the deepening shadows. Soon the windows of the great house showed golden through the trees.

"You can imagine what this place was like in the old days," said Madame Yasnova wistfully.

Kate could. She could picture it all. She could almost hear the music of the waltzes and polkas and mazurkas that had once floated out through those windows into the scented night – almost see the floating, whirling balldresses, the gorgeous uniforms of the officers as they spun their partners round those gleaming floors under the sparkling chandeliers.

Madame Yasnova must have guessed her thoughts. "There was much suffering, much evil

73

in Tsarist days," she said softly. "We all know that a revolution was inevitable. Yet there is a great interest among our younger generation in that period, a nostalgia, I think, for the elegance that has passed away."

"It's the same with us. Some of my friends are absolutely crazy about anything Victorian."

"It is a natural reaction. There is so much that is ugly and violent in modern life. One sighs for a little gentleness and grace. Our girls demand sex-equality – why not? – yet they are still thrilled when the boys bring them flowers! They still do, you know. Do they in Britain?"

"Not much," said Kate regretfully. No boy had ever brought her flowers.

The Yasnovs saw them to the guest-block. Thank-yous and good-nights were said. Climbing the stairs Dr Holford said, "She really *is* a striking woman."

"Isn't she? She said she'd wanted to go on the stage. I suppose marrying Dr Yasnov . . ."

"It wasn't marrying him that stopped her. She was his patient, very young – at twelve, I think. If it hadn't been for him she wouldn't be alive today."

"How extraordinary!" Kate exclaimed.

"Even he couldn't give her the stamina she needed for the theatre training. It's a tough pro-fession. But he saved her life. I don't think any other doctor could have done it at that time. For-tunately, they fell in love. Fortunately, I'm sure, for both of them."

"I – I think I understand better now." They

paused at her door. "It's been rather a wonderful evening," she said, giving him a good-night kiss.

She walked into her room and switched on the light. Instantly she saw the flowers. Yellow roses, which someone had thoughtfully placed in an earthenware pot. Tilted against it was a cheap envelope, addressed in purple ink. She tore it open.

Dear Miss Holford, it began very formally. We were all so sorry that we did not see you this morning. We waited a long time, then decided that you had been prevented by some other commitment. Later, by chance, we saw you on a yacht, and we argued a great deal, not sure what to think.

"Oh, dear!" Kate gasped under her breath.

For my part I could not believe that you had preferred the company of the rich Americans. I felt sure there was a good reason why you had not kept your promise. We so want to be friends. If you also wish it, and if you are free tomorrow afternoon, we shall be at the café from three o'clock. If you come, please do not let the others know that I have written this letter – let it seem accidental. Kostya would make jokes and my sister would say that I should have left it to her. Your friend, if you will permit it,

The signature was as formal as the opening:
S. P. Ushinsky.

Impulsively she buried her hot face in the cool fragrance of the roses. How delightfully old-world! Stepan was rather a dear.

Altogether, it had been quite a day.

EIGHT

At breakfast Kate learnt with relief that her father would not be needing her that day.

So nothing should prevent her getting to the café. She would have been desperate otherwise. Stepan's letter bore no address, she did not know his telephone number if his family had one, and public telephone directories seemed to be unknown in Russia.

Meanwhile she had to get through the morning. She decided on a swim in the pool, and then perhaps a laze in the grounds, catching up on the long Russian novel she had to finish before the university term began.

Some of the young patients were already disporting themselves in the pool under the supervision of two nurses. She made for the far side, where it was deeper, stripped to her bikini and dived in. The cool water was a delight, just what she had been longing for. She came up, swam a few strokes, then paused, dashing the water from her eyes. This side of the pool proved not quite so deserted as she had thought.

A dark little head broke the surface near her. Two lively dark eyes fixed her with a fascinated gaze.

"May I speak to you, lady? You are English, yes?" The boy addressed her in that language.

She laughed. "I am. Good guess!"

"Then I think you are the daughter of the nice

English doctor – Dr Yasnov brought him to see me in the ward."

"And what's your name?"

"Benjamin. Benjamin Abramovitch Shapiro."

"Hiya, Ben! I'm Kate Holford."

"Hiya. . ." He hesitated. "Kate?" he added doubtfully, his brown face eager and timid at the same time. "You permit I call you 'Kate'?"

"Sure, why not?" She nearly asked him how long he was here for, but remembered, as a doctor's daughter, that it was a dangerous question to ask. Instead, she said, "How long have you been here?"

"It is now almost two years."

"Two years!" she echoed, full of compassion. She could not guess at the nature of his disability. In the water he was as agile as a seal. She said cautiously, "Is the treatment doing you good?"

"Oh, yes!" His confidence was touching. "Dr Yasnov warned us it would be a slow process. He is a wonderful man." The liquid eyes shone even more brightly.

"He certainly is."

She had seen the patchwork of snapshots covering a whole wall in his consulting room. Each photo showed a happy smiling child, playing with friends, busy with a hobby, or just snuggling up blissfully to a parent. Each recorded the successful solution of some ghastly health problem – a cure, or at least a partial cure – after lengthy treatment. She remembered a bright-looking twelve-year-old girl who had undergone seventy operations.

Dr Yasnov was not a conceited man. He did

not keep that picture gallery to boast of his triumphs. He kept it to sustain his own faith and that of his staff. Most of all he kept it to hearten the desperate parents who came to him with cases that everyone else pronounced hopeless.

"I am so lucky to be here," Ben told her solemnly. "You cannot know how lucky."

And you very much want to tell me, she thought. It was hard to carry on a conversation in the water. He showed no inclination to leave her and rejoin the splashing, screaming crowd. So she climbed out, saying, "I want to get some sun." She knew he would come and sit on the grass beside her. He did. "And why are you specially lucky?" she asked.

"Our doctor at home said, 'Ben has only one chance, the Gaidar Sanatorium.' He said, 'Dr Yasnov is a miracle man – but, in the circumstances, I do not think he would dare to accept your son.' "

"Dare?" Kate knitted her brows. Out of the water Ben walked with some awkwardness, but there was nothing else visibly wrong with that suntanned little body. He did not look like a hopeless case.

The reason turned out to be non-medical.

"My father was in disgrace. He was a scientist – he *is* a scientist," Ben corrected himself with defiant emphasis. "But he has lost his employment. He wished to take us all to Israel, to join our relatives there. He was refused a visa to go. They said he could not be permitted to leave the country – in his work he must have learnt defence secrets. It

79

was nonsense. My father had nothing to do with defence. If he had known secrets he would never have betrayed them to another country. He argued too much – he is a great arguer," said Ben with a mixture of pride and regret. "In the end they took away his job. Yet still he was not allowed to emigrate."

Kate nodded sympathetically. She had heard of such cases.

"My father is now a non-person," Ben continued fiercely. "So I am the son of a non-person. But our doctor was mistaken. My father applied to Dr Yasnov. I have told you, he is a great arguer." He chuckled. "But he did not have to argue with Dr Yasnov. Dr Yasnov *insisted* on accepting me. My father has told me, since. Even this great doctor met with much opposition, he risked his own career over my case. He was up against a very powerful man in the Communist Party – and Dr Yasnov is not even a Party member. So he was in a very weak position against this other man . . ."

"Not – Shulgin?" she queried softly.

The boy nodded. "Anatoly Shulgin. He hates Jews."

It was extraordinary, she thought, that wretched man cropped up everywhere! But was it really so extraordinary? He was the big noise in these parts, his influence spread like octopus tentacles. So, even after he had failed to block Dr Yasnov's original appointment, he had used the case of this innocent boy to continue his feud. No wonder Madame Yasnova loathed him.

A hand-bell jangled from the other side of the

pool. The children were clustering, a nurse was filling mugs.

Benjamin stood up, making a face. "I must go. It is time for my milk."

"Nice to have met you, Ben. See you!"

He limped reluctantly away, dived into the water, and struck out across the pool. Poor little scrap, she thought, I must ask Dad about him.

Now she could slip out of her bikini into shorts and T-shirt. She decided to find the Grand Duke's Staircase and take a look at the cove.

She passed the other pools, the "Caspian" with its model boats, the "Aral Sea" full of squealing toddlers. She started down a yew avenue she thought she remembered from last night. A sudden instinct made her look round.

Yes, she *was* being followed. A shadowy small figure was flitting along jerkily under the trees. She felt mildly irritated, she wanted to get on to the cove, not be slowed down by a chattering child, but she had not the heart to ignore him.

He was so pathetically anxious to talk to her. She wondered, was he cold-shouldered by the other children? Or was he too clever for most of them? Was he longing to stretch his mind in older company?

She waited for him to catch up with her. They went on together, but more slowly.

Ben was certainly a remarkably knowledgeable boy. He knew the names of these rare exotic trees which the Grand Duke had collected from all over the world. Last night, Kate had seen them only as dim brooding shapes. Even now, in the brilliant morning daylight, she could not have identified a quarter of the isolated specimen trees that dotted the park. Ben had their names pat, and their countries of origin, Chile or China, Java or Japan.

"I don't know how you do it," she confessed.

"It is nothing," he said airily. "When I knew I should be here for a long time I made up my mind. There is a book in the library. One must do something."

They were nearing the place where the path led off to the cove. "This is what I was looking out for," she said. "This peculiar rock slab. I don't know what it was ever meant to be."

But, of course, this surprising child did. "It is an anchor, Kate, a ship's anchor."

"An *anchor*?"

"From the Bronze Age. My father showed me one like this in a museum – when I was just a little boy." The last phrase made her struggle to keep a straight face. "They are not uncommon," he said casually. "They are naturally more durable than an iron anchor. See, the cable ran through this hole." He ran his finger over some lines cut deep into the stone. "This symbol —"

"What is it?"

"The museum label said it was the crude outline of a ship's rudder."

"You remember even the label – after years?"

"I can always remember what interests me." He was not smug, simply truthful.

"What a funny place for an anchor, up here! But the Grand Duke seems to have collected

82

anything if it looked ancient enough."

"He was not, I think, very scientific," said Ben with deep disapproval.

A few yards along the path the ground fell sharply away at their feet. Rock steps went zigzagging dizzily down to the cove. There had been handrails once. Now only short stretches remained.

"You must not come down," she ordered.

"I can manage —"

"No, Ben." It would be too terrible if anything happened. "Sorry, but it's too dangerous."

"Dr Yasnov says it is good for me to attempt things."

"But not this. You must promise me – you will sit down on this top step and not move till I come up again."

"Oh, *Kate* —"

"Promise! Or we shall have to turn round and go straight back. And I don't want to. But if you make me," she threatened, "I shan't speak a word to you – we shall walk in silence."

That did the trick. He sat down meekly. He was not too sorry to sit down, she suspected. They had covered some distance. He needed a rest.

She went down the Grand Duke's Staircase. It was crumbly in places, but safe enough for a normally fit person.

The cove was an enchanted place. A slender cascade splashed down from above; in the winter it would be a quite impressive torrent. Bygone landslides had tumbled huge boulders higgledy-piggledy into the shallows, and over the centuries stormy waves had worn them smooth.

It would be quite possible to swim, and safe to dive if you chose the spot carefully. Peering into the transparent water she saw that it deepened rapidly. There might be a nasty cold current where the cascade plunged down. And if one ventured unwisely beyond the mouth of the cove the sheer cliffs outside might give one no chance to struggle ashore again.

She climbed back to the tiny waving figure silhouetted against a white cloud.

"Was it beautiful down there?" he asked wistfully as she sank down breathless beside him.

"*Very* beautiful."

"I think also a little mysterious?"

She laughed. "Why mysterious?"

He shrugged. "I do not know, but . . ." He stopped.

It seems mysterious to him, she thought sympathetically, because it is unattainable. I would not let him go down with me.

"We should be getting back." She jumped up, took his hand, and pulled him to his feet. "Come on."

They chattered all the way back to the sanatorium. He bombarded her with questions about the outside world which, for his father as well as himself, had been so far unattainable. She answered his questions as well as she could, but with only half her mind.

She was already thinking about those other friends she was hoping to see in the afternoon.

NINE

Kate spotted them at the café before they saw her. Marina was describing something with giggles and animated gestures. Kostya was one huge grin as he listened to her, the white sticking-plaster still conspicuous on his nose. Stepan sat with long legs sprawled, his eyes roving over the crowd in the opposite direction.

With heart in mouth, but courage in both hands, she made for their table under the trees.

"I'm so glad I saw you!" she burst out breathlessly. "I want to explain about yesterday."

"Sit down!" cried Kostya. He jumped up and seized another chair from the next table.

"And how have you been getting on?" asked Marina in a neutral tone.

"I want to tell you. My father needed me yesterday morning. I couldn't get here in time."

"I told them so," said Stepan triumphantly. "I was sure you would have come if you had been able."

"But what must you have thought when you saw me on that yacht with those Americans?"

There was a brief but awkward silence. Kostya said, "Oh – was that *you*?" His surprise was unconvincing.

"Of course it was! I waved like mad. Why didn't you wave back? You seemed to turn away."

Marina said quickly, in a much friendlier tone,

"There has obviously been a misunderstanding. On both sides. We could not believe it was you."

"Well, it so happens that it was." Kate tried, without complete success, to conceal the hurt in her voice. "If you think I'd break a promise, just because I'd been invited to a yacht, you – you certainly don't know me very well!"

Kostya defused the situation. "But we *want* to, dear Kate. You must forgive us. Please."

"Yes, *please*," said Marina warmly. "What a fortunate coincidence that we have met again like this! Wasn't it, Stepan?" she demanded pointedly, fixing her brother with a glint of amused suspicion in her eye.

"You will have coffee?" asked Stepan hastily. "I'll catch the waitress." He turned away to hide his confusion. To help him, Kate said, "I thought I'd try the café on the off chance. I thought, if you came here regularly —"

"It was a happy thought," said Marina with a dead pan expression.

Kate continued her explanation of yesterday. They understood, of course: she had had to go to the meeting with her father. They saw now that she could not possibly have kept her date with them in time. But the yacht and all those Americans called for further explanation. She told them of her encounter with Pearl Hathaway, and why, as she had missed them, she had accepted the invitation to the yacht.

"I'd have done the same," Marina assured her.

Kate guessed that they now felt a little guilty for having misjudged her. Yet their instinctive reaction, on seeing her from the quay, had been natural enough. They had jumped to the false conclusion that she had deserted them in favour of a more tempting offer – they had probably imagined the yacht and its occupants as more glamorous than they were.

She began to tell them about the rather boring party. Suddenly Kostya broke in. "Here he is! Here's Peter!" He flung up an arm and signalled.

The man threading his way between the other tables was of nondescript appearance. He was noticeable only because he was in the early stages of growing a beard, which, thought Kate, made anyone look scruffy. He seemed a few years older than the others.

Kostya introduced him as "Peter the Pirate". Kate took this as a reference to the fierce black stubble sprouting from his jaw, but Marina quickly explained.

"Most visitors stay in holiday homes run by their trade unions or whatever – it's so much cheaper. But it's more official and, well, organ-ized. So some people like to make their own arrangements – stay with friends, perhaps, or in private lodgings." She laughed. "We call them 'pirates'."

"I like to be independent," said the newcomer, whose real name was Peter Polyanov. He did not say what his "own arrangements" were, and Marina later explained to Kate that none of them knew. Peter was not shy, but reserved. They had met him on the beach just as they had met Kate herself. They found him very agreeable, but they did not press him with personal questions.

That must be a strain, thought Kate, for Russians loved asking personal questions, especially about one's family. As soon as Peter had ordered his coffee it was her own turn to be cross-examined. Marina demanded photographs. She had to turn out her wallet for snapshots of her parents and the rest of the family.

Too late she realized that mixed up with them was a photo of Henry, sent with his last letter. She tried to slip it out of sight, but Peter detected her clumsy attempt and laid his finger on the print.

"You have forgotten to tell us of this one!"

"It is someone special, yes?" cried Kostya gleefully.

Kate was embarrassed. It might have been better to explain Henry quite truthfully – a school friend, whose photo in her wallet had been a mere accident. Too late for that now. Their curiosity was roused. But her feelings – her non-feelings – about Henry were no business of theirs. She decided to tease them, as they deserved to be teased, for being so nosy.

"Special?" she echoed. "I suppose you could say so."

"Ha!" exclaimed Kostya.

"If a brother is 'special'," she said.

Kostya studied the photograph. "He is not much like you," he said suspiciously.

Marina came to her support. "*I* am not much like Stepan – I hope."

Kate thought this a little unkind to Stepan. But she smiled and answered, "There's an English saying, 'Beauty is in the eye of the beholder'."

"Very true," said Kostya slyly, "or in the sex of the beholder!"

"Go on telling us about the Americans and their yacht," said Stepan hastily.

Kate was only too glad to resume her story. They were all much intrigued by the eccentric Mr Flann and his obsession with the myths and legends of the Black Sea.

"Did you like him, this man?" Marina asked.

"I – I'm not sure."

"Why not?"

Kate groped for the right Russian word but could not find it. "There were moments when he seemed a bit – what we call – 'phony'."

"How?" Peter spoke very softly.

"Well, as I've said, he didn't claim to be an expert, but he made one or two surprising slips. As if he hadn't genuinely studied the subject, just mugged it up in a superficial way. I remember once at school," Kate smiled at the memory, "the history teacher was ill – someone else had to stand in for her at short notice. The other teacher didn't know his stuff but he wouldn't admit it. We could tell he was just mugging it up from the book the night before, so we laid traps for him. We were awful little horrors, I suppose."

They listened entranced. "I do not think we should dare to treat our teachers so," said Marina enviously.

"I don't want to be unfair to Mr Flann," said Kate. "I admire people who teach themselves. We can't all get to university, and many of us don't want to. But if a person *is* crazy on some subject he does usually end by knowing all about it. He doesn't make elementary mistakes."

"True," agreed Kostya.

"I mean, *I've* no background myself, only the bits of general knowledge you need in a quiz, but even I could see that he was wrong on some points."

"Such as?" Peter's nondescript appearance was deceptive. Behind it, Kate guessed, was a very acute mind.

"He was holding forth about the Roman poet Ovid. He was exiled to the Black Sea coast. He'd offended the emperor. He had to live in a remote place called Tomi, away from all his friends in Rome. Mr Flann got rather sentimental about how miserable he must have been. He told us how sad he'd felt himself, wandering over the ground today, feeling very close to the spirit of poor old Ovid, fancying he heard his voice in the rustle of the trees – all that sort of blah. Only —"

"Only?" Peter prompted her.

"He talked about Ovid pleading with Julius Caesar to pardon him."

"Well?"

"You see, it wasn't Julius Caesar who'd exiled him. It was his great-nephew, the emperor Augustus Caesar. Actually, Julius never was emperor. Even I knew that," said Kate, "so Mr Flann certainly should have done."

"Had he been to Tomi?"

"He gave the impression he had. Saying how he'd wandered over the desolate site, meditating what it must have been like in those days. It's in Romania now."

"It is indeed." Peter broke into a smile, teeth flashing white through the beginnings of his beard. "But your Mr Flann can hardly have wandered over the desolate site, listening to ghostly voices in the trees. Moaning in Latin, presumably – which I gather Mr Flann would not understand in any case."

They all laughed.

"Tomi is hardly desolate now. Any Roman remains must have been built over long ago. I think Mr Flann has not realized that the Roman Tomi is the city we now call Constanza. It is the chief port of Romania, miles of wharfs and oil pipelines, all bustle and noise. No one could possibly meditate there. I know, for I have been there. Even for a self-educated enthusiast it is a strange gap in Mr Flann's knowledge."

Kate was delighted with this fresh evidence confirming her hunch that there was something not quite convincing about the American's obsession. She warmed to Peter. But she saw from the faces of the others that they were getting lost in this discussion of ancient history. Anxious not to be a bore, she switched to a more topical aspect of her story.

"There was something else a bit odd, yesterday, something quite different." She told them of Shulgin's sudden arrival after they had reached the open sea.

"Shulgin?" demanded Peter. "Who then is this Shulgin?"

The other Russians exclaimed in chorus at his ignorance.

"He's our local boss," said Stepan.

"Up to a year or two ago you would have seen his portrait everywhere," said Marina with deep disgust. "Most of them have been taken down now – we are supposed to have given up 'the cult of personality', leaders are not to be flattered and idolized. But Shulgin remains as powerful as ever. He wields a tremendous amount of influence, but he is more discreet about it."

"He's a dangerous man to cross," said Stepan.

"Tell me more," Peter encouraged him. "I love gossip. The more scandalous the better!"

Now that doesn't ring quite true, thought Kate with surprise. I'd have thought he was the last kind of person to waste time on idle chit chat. Still, he'd said it himself. And he was eyeing Stepan almost hungrily.

Stepan was hesitating. Marina had laid a restraining hand upon his arm. An unwelcome thought came into Kate's head. Was Marina, like Dr Yasnov last night, still uncertain about the safety of free speech? Of course, they didn't *know* much about Peter, he was a chance acquaintance on the beach, didn't belong to this region, had no conceivable motive for running off and telling tales, but . . .

It was an awkward pause. She plunged in to save the situation. She at least, as a foreigner, could speak her mind fearlessly. No one could touch *her*.

She told them about Ben and how Shulgin had

tried to use his admission to the sanatorium as a weapon in his vendetta against Dr Yasnov. She took care not to reveal that the Yasnovs themselves had discussed Shulgin.

"But this was some time ago, surely?" said Peter. "I do not think such things are possible now."

"Don't you believe it," said Stepan. He ignored his sister's warning frown. He was determined to speak out. "The man just has to be more careful now, that's all. You can't get rid of your opponents as they did in Stalin's time – and a good while afterwards. Trump up a false accusation, get them sent to the labour camps – or a mental home! You have to be more subtle these days."

Peter still did not look convinced. "Do you think he had some reason to cover up his connection with this mad American?"

"I don't know. But, as Kate says, he didn't go on board openly in the harbour. Make what you like of that."

Peter laughed. "I think we are making a very fine story out of it."

"You don't see anything odd?" said Kate.

He shrugged. "How should I know?"

"Is there no corruption still where *you* live?" Stepan challenged him.

Peter was not to be drawn. "How should I know?" he repeated. He yawned. "I am on holiday."

"So are we all," said Marina. She took the opportunity to change the subject before they started an argument. "We should be thinking of

93

our English guest. What can we do to make her stay with us enjoyable?" She turned to Kate with a questioning smile. "Do you like mountains? We could take you up the highest one in the Crimea. It is something to remember – to stand on Ai-Petri at dawn and see the sunrise! There is a funicular," she added encouragingly.

Her brother exploded. "A funicular! Kate does not want to stand amid a gaping crowd." He turned to her. "All the tourists are encouraged to go there. There is a war memorial to the Crimean partisans who fought the Nazis. It is a place of pilgrimage. Fine! But for the sunrise let us take you to a place where you can see it just as well, without the multitude. It will be the same sunrise. You like walking?"

"I love it."

Stepan knew a truck-driver who regularly made the trip along the coast road at night, fetching fresh produce. For a small tip he would give them a lift so far. Then there was a track leading up to a spur that made a splendid viewpoint over the sea.

Marina said, "But would your father —"

"It'll be OK with Dad," Kate said easily. She had more than once gone for all-night hikes with her friends.

"The moon will be full next week," said Stepan. "You'll be here still, Peter? When does your holiday end?"

"I shall be here," Peter assured him.

"Just a moment!" Kate had a disturbing thought. "My father has a medical conference in Odessa. He might want me." She pulled out her pocket diary and they all waited anxiously. She brightened. "No, it's all right. Odessa's the week after."

"Excellent," said Stepan. "Leave it all to me."

Marina said mockingly, "My brother is very capable – capable of anything!"

"And now," said Kostya standing up, "we go for a swim?"

As they left the café Kate managed to whisper to Stepan her thanks for the roses. "They're lovely."

"Not only the roses," he murmured back.

TEN

Waiting in the dark at the roadside, Kate had the pleasant sense of an adventure about to begin.

They talked instinctively in low voices, though they were doing nothing illegal. It seemed a black night for mountain-walking but Stepan promised that the moon would soon be up.

Igor, his truck-driving friend, had preferred to pick them up here, outside the town. She guessed that he was not supposed to give people lifts.

"He makes the trip every night," said Stepan, "collecting fresh fruit and vegetables. The truck's empty, going out. What harm if he takes us the first few kilometres?"

After a late supper at a café they had walked eastwards along the coast road climbing steeply out of the town. At first, looking back, they could see the lights glittering along the sea front, and others like coloured beads, on the moored vessels and craft gliding to and fro on the open sea beyond. Now, though, they had turned a shoulder of the mountain. The lights below were blotted out. There were only the white stars overhead.

At this hour there was little traffic. When they heard the labouring of a heavy vehicle, and saw the long fingers of its headlights slanting upwards against the cypresses, Stepan announced confidently, "Here he comes!"

He stepped forward with upraised arm. The

lorry stopped. Igor, seemingly a young man of few words, called out a terse greeting and waved them into the back of the truck. It was by no means empty – half its space was stacked with cardboard boxes – but there was ample room for the five of them. Peter the Pirate had come as promised, though he had not joined them in many of their activities during the past week. He did not like to be tied down.

They scrambled into the truck. Kate felt Stepan's hands on her hips, lightly swinging her up. They settled themselves as best they could. Igor drove off.

The road still climbed. "We are two hundred metres above the sea," said Stepan. "It will save us a lot of time and effort." After a little while they stopped with a jerk. He leant forward and shouted, "No, Igor – not here."

"This is not for you." Igor dropped from the cab and came round to the rear. "I am sorry, I must disturb you."

The cartons apparently had to be unloaded here, although strangely there was no sign of any building. Kate stood up with the others and helped to hand down the cartons. They clinked, but the bottles inside were obviously empty. Under Igor's direction the young men soon had them all stacked behind a clump of bushes. The headlights showed a narrow path slanting up into a vineyard. No doubt someone would eventually come down to collect the cartons.

They got back into the truck, Stepan as helpful

as before. As they drove on, he was watchful for the sharp bends, his arm ready to save Kate from being violently flung about.

"The road is very zigzag," he whispered apologetically.

There were so many bends and from the back of the lorry it was impossible to see them coming. It seemed sensible not to remove his arm, and Kate saw no need to hurt his feelings by detaching herself.

Soon – almost too soon – Igor pulled up again.

"This is it," said Stepan. He leapt out and spread his arms wide. She jumped and he caught her. Kostya helped Marina. Peter followed, a light-footed shadow.

They called their thanks to Igor. The tail-light of the truck bobbed away and they were alone.

"Oh, look," cried Marina, "the moon!"

Eastwards, the sea was suddenly all aglitter. The full moon was low on the horizon, but rising – rising, thought Kate, from the deserts of central Asia, leaping the mountain wall of the fabled Caucasus, lighting up the coastal lands of Medea and her wicked witchcraft, Jason and the Golden Fleece. . . After her meeting with Flann the associations sprang readily to mind. This was a night for poetry.

"Come on," said Stepan briskly, "we've a long climb in front of us."

He started up a track that ran steeply upwards between the vine-terraces. At times he turned and stretched out a helping hand to Kate.

"Your shoes are not good," he said sternly.

"Sorry. They're the best I have with me."

The airline baggage allowance had not covered ideal equipment for every occasion. She had not expected to be toiling up a stony track in the middle of the night with a young man she had not known until a week ago.

Kostya and Marina were twenty metres behind, laughing and talking softly. Peter, odd man out as usual, brought up the rear.

Kate and Stepan did not talk much. It was difficult, panting upwards in single file, and somehow did not seem necessary. The frequent contact of hands, her own warm fingers engulfed in Stepan's strong paw as he steadied her over a rough patch, was all they needed.

The moon was climbing too. The whole landscape was suffused with a luminous silver light. The half-grown grapes gleamed like pearls as they dangled on the vines.

All my life, thought Kate with a sudden poignant certainty – whatever lies ahead of me – I shall remember this night.

She was almost sorry, despite aching legs and thumping heart, when Stepan paused on a level shelf of ground and waited for the others.

He pointed out landmarks. The stark cliffs of Orliny Zalyat, the sweeping bay below Gurzuf, where they had been yesterday to see the Pushkin Museum, and the massive hump of Bear Mountain, Ayu-Dag.

"It *does* look like a bear," she agreed. "Bending down to drink from the sea."

They sat down for a brief rest.

Peter broke in upon her poetic mood with a grim reminder of recent history. "Must have been good guerrilla country here."

"It was," agreed Stepan. "Our partisans led the Nazis a fine old dance." In case Kate did not know, he added, "All the Crimea was overrun by Hitler's armies for a time."

"But there was underground resistance?" said Peter.

"You bet! Often literally underground."

"You mean caves?"

"And the old abandoned wine-cellars. Passages running into the mountainside. Like mine-workings. Good hiding places."

"But death-traps if the enemy found them!"

"True enough."

"Not pleasant," said Peter thoughtfully. "They'd only have to creep up to the entrance and lob a few grenades into them —"

"Oh, let's not talk about such horrible things tonight," Marina pleaded.

They resumed their climb. The vineyards gave place to forest, oaks and beeches. And then, as the pale track mounted ever higher through the gloom, sombre and mysterious pines with an occasional open patch where slender birches rose like silver wands in the moonlight. Once they startled some deer, which flitted away before them and in a moment were gone.

This is *dreamy*, thought Kate. But she could not express her feeling in Russian and was not sure that she wanted to. She was content to tread silently at Stepan's heels. The pine-needles muted their footsteps.

Overhead, through the breaks in the treetops, the sky was growing pale. When they emerged from the forest the stars had gone and the moon was a faint disc.

"Soon be dawn," murmured Stepan.

"And time for coffee," said Kostya hopefully.

"When we get there." Stepan was firm. Kostya groaned.

They were not trying to reach the highest altitudes, which went up to six hundred metres. But Stepan had a good viewpoint in mind.

After the forest they were in alpine meadows, rolling down from the crinkled escarpment which hemmed the skyline above. A tiny stream came gurgling down, hardly visible among the wild flowers and grasses. It was their only guide, for the path had petered out. The water came cascading down from a deep cleft in the rock.

"Here," said Stepan. He slipped off the backpack in which he was carrying most of their provisions.

Kate sank down thankfully on a boulder. Looking back, they could see across the fringe of treetops to the sea far beyond. The sky now was turning pink. A pool at the foot of the cascade reflected it in gleams of rose.

Peter stood, looking seawards, a pair of binoculars glued to his eyes. "Kate," he called. "That is your American's yacht, I think?"

She jumped up as he held out the binoculars.

At first she could make out only a thin streak, like a stick. Never having studied the vessel from a distance, she could not have recognized its outline.

"Could be," she admitted.

Even with Peter's powerful binoculars it was impossible to tell if the flag was Turkish or Soviet. Both were red, both carried a star. Whether the flag bore a crescent also, or a hammer and sickle, was uncertain at that distance.

Peter appeared less doubtful. "An unusual hour for pleasure craft to be at sea," he commented. "But presumably your Mr Flann has his own good reasons."

Remembering Flann, Kate felt quite sure he would have his reasons – whether they were "good" or not. Her mind went back to that conversation with the Yasnovs. There had been rumours once that Flann was an American spy, using his supposed passion for the scenes of Greek mythology to collect up-to-date intelligence about the coastline. In which case, where did Shulgin come in? Could Shulgin be a traitor to his own country, feeding information to the American? Flann could just as easily be a double agent.

It was all very bewildering. Probably just a wild fancy, anyhow. It would be unwise to say anything to her Russian friends.

Marina looked up from setting out the breakfast on a flat slab of rock. "I'm glad someone has binoculars."

"It is to study birds," Peter explained quickly.

She laughed in surprise. "I never suspected —"

"Suspected?" He snatched at the word defensively.

"That you were a bird-watcher. We're constantly finding out new things about you." Marina was fond of teasing him. But he could be as prickly, thought Kate, as that awful beard he was growing.

"I am only a beginner, Marina, you must not expect me to answer questions —"

"No one would ever expect you to answer questions!"

"On birds, I mean." He was floundering. "Your Crimean birds are different from those we have at home." Still he dropped no clue as to where his home was.

"Yes," agreed Marina, "I believe we still have eagles and vultures in these mountains."

"And grouse," Stepan contributed, "and capercailzie."

"I should like to see a capercailzie," said Peter with every show of interest. But Kate wondered whether he would know a capercailzie from a crow or a cormorant.

What an odd person he was! Why had he tacked himself on to this little group? It could hardly be the ordinary loneliness of a solitary holidaymaker. He seemed to have other friends – or acquaintances anyhow – in Yalta. She had seen him break off to speak to them on the beach or in a café – though, being Peter he had never introduced them. And anyhow he said that solitude appealed to him. Perhaps on the days when they did not see him he really was bird-watching, but she found that hard to believe.

"Breakfast!" announced Marina.

"Thank heaven!" said Kostya.

The coffee was poor stuff. It tasted as though – as often in Russia – it had been eked out with dandelion. Even so it was as welcome to Kate as it was to the others. She never took sugar, so that shortage did not trouble her. There was honey, however, to spread on the thick slices of rye bread. "From Babushka's own beehives," said Stepan. Babushka, or "Granny", lived in a cottage just above the town. Kate must meet Babushka.

"I'd love to."

The hard-boiled eggs had also come from Babushka's hens. Kostya had brought salami and garlic sausage. Peter, that man of surprises, had somehow managed to buy a bottle of sparkling wine. Everyone exclaimed, for the Government's crack down on alcohol had created long queues for such supplies as were available. Peter cooled the bottle in the stream while they drank their coffee, and then opened it expertly with a pop that echoed from the rocks like a gun shot.

"Crimean champagne!" he said as he poured it frothing into their cups. "From your own Massandra vineyards."

It would have been too sweet for her father's taste, thought Kate, but the Russians liked everything sweet, and she herself was too inexperienced to be critical. They all drank a laughing toast to Apollo, the sun god, as he came over the eastern horizon in a blaze of gold.

Stepan smiled at her. "It was worth the long walk?"

"Oh, *yes*! Thank you!"

Peter was scanning the sea again. But the *Meltemi* had disappeared about its business – whatever that business might be. There were only some fishing boats. "I had hoped," he said "that we might see the coast of Asia Minor."

"We're not high enough here," said Stepan. "You can from Ai-Petri – on a clear day."

"I'm not so sure it's going to be very clear," said his sister.

The sky was changing rapidly. After that splendid sunrise, curtains of cloud were racing across. Their upper edges shone gold where they caught the sun that had vanished behind them, but their bellying undersides were ominously black.

"I think we'd better be getting down," said Stepan. "It's unusual at this time of year. But our Black Sea storms can come up quite suddenly."

"It *does* look threatening," said Kate wistfully. "But rather grand."

Marina was bundling the picnic things into Stepan's pack. He slipped it on again, pulled Kate to her feet. "Come on, it's best not to be caught up here."

They filed down across the flower-spangled mountainside at a trot. The pinewood seemed even gloomier than it had done in the twilight before dawn. The rain was now pattering overhead. Stray drops splashed upon them. When they got down among the oaks and beeches, the rain was slackening. They paused under the fringe of dripping branches.

"I hope it will pass," said Marina.

They debated briefly. Should they wait here, or push on downhill through the exposed vineyards? Once on the road, they might get a lift to Yalta.

They decided to go on. "After all, we wanted spectacular cloud effects," said Kostya cheerfully.

They were certainly getting them. The massive storm-clouds were rolling up like the breakers of an angry sea.

"So long as it doesn't thunder," panted Marina. She sounded nervous.

But the thunder came all too soon, with a blinding flash of lightning and a terrifying sizzling crash like an explosion.

The rain was hissing down again. The vines gave no more protection than a screen of lace. Kate was soaked to the skin. But the thunder and lightning worried her more on this exposed mountainside. She hurtled down the slope behind Stepan.

He shouted over his shoulder, "I know somewhere —"

Another cataclysmic crash drowned whatever else he was saying.

Hailstones drummed. Branched lightning flickered, blue-grey, like steel.

She stumbled as a vine tendril caught her ankle. She regained her balance, continued her headlong rush.

"Here!" Stepan's arm barred her passage. He

swung her lightly to one side. "In here – quick!"

There was level ground under her feet, cover of some sort overhead, a musty smell in her nostrils. The thunder still crashed, but somehow it was now muted.

The others pressed close behind her, breathless and dripping. From behind Peter asked, "Where on earth are we?"

Stepan answered from the darkness. "We're not *on* earth, we're under it. Which is safer – and drier – at the moment. One of those old wine-stores I was telling you about. Just right, till this storm blows over."

Peter, needless to say, had a pocket-torch, and he flashed it round. They were standing in a sort of tunnel, running straight into the mountain.

"They don't seem to have left any of their wine," said Kostya ruefully. "I bet nobody's been here for years and years."

"And that," said Peter in a curious tone, "is just where I think you may be quite mistaken."

ELEVEN

"What do you mean?" asked Kostya.

"Well, Stepan's been here before," Peter pointed out, a trifle impatiently.

"Yes, I stumbled on it with some other boys. I suppose, oh, five years ago."

"But these cigarettes weren't smoked five years ago." Peter was flashing his torch over the rocky floor of the tunnel. Several white cigarette-ends trailed away into the inner darkness. Russian cigarettes, Kate had noticed, had tobacco for only half their length – the rest was empty paper cylinder, which meant that cigarette-ends were long and conspicuous. These also looked comparatively clean and fresh.

"So what?" Marina demanded. "Other people have sheltered here, the same as us."

"The weather has been perfect for weeks." Peter turned to Stepan. "Is the tunnel obvious from outside?"

"No, the entrance is screened by a lot of prickly bushes."

"You're telling me," said Marina with feeling. "It was like forcing your way through a hedge. Where are you off to, Peter?" He was walking further into the tunnel, his torch-beam ranging up and down, right and left.

"Just poking about," he called back. "I'm a little curious."

"I do wish he *wasn't* so curious," Marina

whispered to Kate crossly. "Why can't we stay here till the storm's passed over? I don't like this kind of place. It's spooky."

Peter continued his advance into the heart of the mountain. The other young men followed. "I'm not staying here in the pitch dark," said Marina shakily. Nobody else had brought a torch, so they could only hurry to overtake the light bobbing away in front of them.

"Wait for us!" Marina pleaded. There was a hint of panic in her wail. "We can't see where we're putting our feet. We might fall down some hole or —"

"Don't be an idiot," said her brother, but he was chivalrous enough to turn back for them. "It's all perfectly safe. You see too many films."

"It's all right for you," said Kate, to defend Marina. "You say *you've* been here before!"

"Not as far inside as this, actually. We were only kids and it *was* a bit scary," Stepan admitted good-humouredly. "We'd no light but a box of matches, and they gave out —"

"So you can't possibly be sure it's safe further on!" said Marina sharply.

"No - except that Peter's in front of us. And he hasn't fallen into an abyss - yet."

Just then Peter called back to them, his voice echoing in the tunnel. "It is widening out now! A big vault, perhaps a cave —"

"Then please wait for us," shouted Stepan.

And Peter meekly answered, "OK."

They went forward again more confidently. The mustiness which had first struck them, after the rain-freshened morning air outside, was no longer noticeable. Even at this distance under-ground the atmosphere was quite wholesome.

"There must have been ventilation shafts when they kept wine here," said Stepan, "and they haven't got blocked up."

They had almost caught up with Peter. He must have heard the last remark for he said, "Talking of wine, someone has broken a bottle here."

They were aware of broken glass now, crunch-ing under their feet. Peter stopped, picked up the jagged neck of a winebottle, and sniffed it.

"No smell, no trace of a label. What does that suggest?"

"Water," said Marina promptly. "Stepan used to wash out an old winebottle and fill it from the tap when he went hiking as a boy. Didn't *you*, ever?"

"Peter would always take champagne," said Kostya.

Peter ignored that. Kate tried to imagine him as a boy, hiking, most likely alone. Reserved, per-haps secretive, already with this compulsion to find mysteries where probably no mystery existed, niggling away at a problem like a puppy with a tangle of string. He had told her that, like many Russians, he loved the Sherlock Holmes stories.

She was standing now in the cave or vault or whatever it was – it was difficult to see whether it was natural or excavated. The stone winebins, stretching away in rows to right and left, like shelves or counters, were obviously man-made.

110

Kate had seen similar bins when she had visited a French vineyard on a family holiday. Only here there were none of the casks or the stacks of horizontal bottles she had seen then.

Peter had moved forward again. "Ah," he called back, "now we are getting somewhere."

He had found a bin crowded with bottles. They stood upright, different shapes and colours, flashing back the gleam of his questing torch – white or green glass, straw-brown or black. He opened one, lifted it to his lips and tasted the contents gingerly. Then he put it down with a wry expression.

"*Samogon!*"

It was a word Kate had learnt only since her arrival in Russia. It was the illegal substitute for vodka, which people were making secretly to defeat the Government's campaign against alcohol.

The Russians had always been heavy drinkers. It caused inefficiency, absenteeism, and dangerous accidents. It cost industry millions in lowered production. But the higher prices and restrictions had only driven the problem underground – in this case, quite literally.

"*Samogon*," repeated the young man. "Our fastest growing industry," he added bitterly.

"I believe it was the same in America," said Kostya. "When they tried complete prohibition many years ago, it led to the bootleggers, gangsters and rackets, gang-warfare and murder. If we are not careful, we shall go the same way."

"It is starting," Marina agreed. "We hear things at the film studios."

They advanced further into the vault. Clearly they had stumbled into a secret distillery. There were bags of grain, sacks of potatoes, many half rotten. Alcohol could be distilled from either. Or from sugar – of which they found long stacks of bags on one of the bins.

"So that's why there are queues in the shops," said Kate. "But how do *these* people get it?"

"Influence," said Stepan. "Influence – in high places."

"And here, I think," said Peter, "is the actual equipment."

To Kate's eye it looked rather like an over-grown version of apparatus she had seen in the lab at school. A retort, a condenser, a flask to receive the distilled liquid through a sloping tube . . . One did not need anything very large-scale or elaborate. She knew that in Ireland – and in Scotland too – country people had often produced their own spirits from such stills to avoid paying tax to the government.

"Only one thing is missing," said Peter.

"What?" asked Kostya.

"Empty bottles for the next batch!"

They all exclaimed together, seeing the obvious connection with those cartons they had helped to stack at the roadside.

"Igor!" cried Marina. "Stepan, your friend must be one of the bootleggers."

"He's not that sort," said Stepan in a troubled voice.

"Innocent people easily get involved," said Peter soothingly. "Then they learn quickly that it is safer not to ask questions. They are afraid."

"I don't blame them," said Kostya. "It is a very rough game. It is better not to know."

A disturbing thought struck Kate. "But *we* know – now."

"Let's get out of here," begged Marina. "I expect the storm is over."

"Well, we have seen enough," said Peter calmly. He seemed to have taken over from Stepan as leader of the party.

They followed him back to the narrow tunnel from which they had come. But they were too late. As they prepared to enter it Peter's guiding light was switched off, leaving them in utter darkness, from which they heard his voice, lowered to a husky warning.

"Someone's coming. Get back. *Quietly.*"

They edged backwards, bumping against each other. He marshalled them somehow, pushing them between the rows of winebins on the right.

"Here. Not a sound!" His whisper was almost inaudible.

They all froze obediently where they stood. Any further retreat would have meant more footsteps, doubled risk of discovery. Kate felt a big hand close round her own and squeeze it. Stepan was next to her. It was a comfort.

She heard noisy, clumping footfalls approaching. Deep voices. Gently Stepan pulled her down into a crouched position. Though she could see nothing she knew that they were all crouching like that, their bowed heads below the level of the bins.

TWELVE

Raising her eyes cautiously, stealing a glance, Kate became aware of a wavering yellow light coming from the tunnel and every moment gathering strength, just as the voices were becoming louder.

She bent her head again. And in that position, almost like kneeling in church, she prayed fervently enough – that these unknown people would not glance sideways as they went by. The first of them had emerged from the tunnel, they were level with that little row of huddled figures between the bins, they were passing by without any pause. . .

With her chin down over her chest, from the corners of her eyes, she could see only legs and boots and the dangling lanterns that some of them carried. Most seemed to be well laden – an occasional clink suggested those boxes of empty bottles – and, as they had to watch where they were going, she hoped they were less likely to turn their heads and look into the surrounding gloom.

The last two men were deep in argument as they drew near.

"Why should *he*? We take the risks."

"Not so much risk. He fixes it for us. Nobody else could."

"But —"

"If you want protection you got to pay for it!"

"But why so much?"

"You know Shulgin."

"Who doesn't?" The speaker sounded bitter, and went on grumbling as they trudged past towards the further end of the cave.

There was a fair amount of hubbub as all the clinking cartons were set down and a buzz of talk began. A brisk voice cut across it. "Come on, lads! Let's get on with it."

Peter whispered. "This is our best chance. Keep close behind me."

Thankfully they straightened up. Unsafe to use the torch. Just the dimmest light filtered down from the lanterns at the far end, where the silhouetted figures of the bootleggers were clustered intently round the still. Stepping with utmost care, the five friends made their shadowy departure into the narrow mouth of the tunnel.

For all their caution some slight noise must have betrayed them. A voice bellowed, "Who's that?"

A second voice yelled, "Stop! Whoever you are, *stop*!"

"Let's get out of here," Marina almost sobbed.

No point in silence now. They crowded into the tunnel, arms spread, hands groping for the walls.

A shot rang out. A bullet screeched along the arched rock over their heads.

Peter stood aside to let the others pass. "I can hold them back for a bit." He was amazingly calm. He had completely taken over now. "Get right away," he ordered. "Fast! I'll see you later."

"But —" Stepan began.

"I'll be all right. Get them *out*."

Peter turned away. Something flashed from his hands. This time the gun's report – so close, and in the confined space of the tunnel – was startling. There was a cry of alarm from the bootleggers. Someone started to shoot back. Dust and rock splinters flew.

"Go," said Peter between his teeth. "For God's sake, go." It was his first sign of desperation.

"Come on, then," said Stepan, and they fled. Behind them the shots cracked to and fro. A bend in the tunnel took them out of danger. Soon a gleam of light showed that they were near the outlet. They were no longer stumbling in the dark.

Marina led. They could run now at full pelt, the rock floor clear beneath their feet.

Kate raced close behind. So Peter had a gun! His rearguard action might enable them to get away. But Peter himself . . .

The outlet showed as a wide white archway of sky. A burly figure rose up against it, arms spread wide.

"What's this? *Girls*?"

Marina screamed as he grasped her. Kate flung herself at him, scrabbling vainly at an arm that was massive and hard as a tree trunk.

Then Stepan was there. His clenched fist caught the bootlegger on the jaw. The man fell backwards, releasing Marina. Both girls went sprawling into the bushes. But whereas they were up again in a moment the man lay inert among the boulders, eyes shut.

"We must do as Peter said," panted Kostya. "Get right away."

"You take the girls down," said Stepan. "I —"

"Don't be a fool. We can't do anything without guns."

"I'll just see . . ."

Stepan bent over the unconscious bootlegger, feeling for a hidden weapon, but there was no sign of any. "He's cracked his head," Stepan grunted. "Look - blood, not much. But if he comes round before Peter gets out —"

"Oh, *do* come on!" begged Marina hysterically.

"You go. And Kate. Kostya, take them down. Quickly. I must tie this chap up - for Peter's sake."

"This'll be quicker - and just as good."

Kostya stooped and tugged at the man's boots. Kate was already bustling Marina down the slope when first one boot, and then a second, came sailing through the air to crash down somewhere among the vines.

A few moments later the two young men caught up with the girls. "*He* won't give Peter much trouble," Kostya assured them, "even if he does come round in time!"

But the look-out man, thought Kate, would be the least of Peter's worries, if that crowd of men were hard on his heels. *They* had guns, some of them anyhow. But, stumbling breathlessly down the terraced mountainside, she could do no more than pray that somehow he would manage to shake them off.

The past hour had changed her view of Peter.

He was no longer nondescript. He was emerging as rather an intriguing character. Fancy his having a gun!

They raced on, pelting down through the vineyard, thankful for the cover of the foliage. After the storm the wet earth steamed under their feet. The grapes shone bright with moisture.

Turning to stare back up the slope she could not see any sign of movement. Indeed, it was already impossible to guess exactly where the tunnel-entrance would be. Nor was there any shouting – or any more shots. But was that good, or did it mean . . .

She could only run on with the others. Now, below them, the coast road wound its snaky way. Once on that, they should be safe.

"Look!" cried Marina joyfully. "Police!"

Small at that distance as a dinky toy, a patrol car was drawn in beside the road.

"What luck!" Help for Peter was at hand. The policemen would have a radio.

But the luck did not hold. As they quickened their pace – Stepan hurtling down the slope quite regardless of his own safety – the uniformed little manikins climbed into their car and drove off. They all yelled, but their voices were lost in the vast emptiness of the mountain air.

Never mind, Kate told herself. Soon they'd be able to raise the alarm. They'd come to a place with a telephone. If not, they'd flag down a passing car.

When they staggered down on to the tarmac ten minutes passed before they saw a vehicle.

Then it was a truck, heaped high with farm produce. They waved frantically, but the driver did not slacken speed. After all, they looked no different from any other hikers, he had a full load, and there were four of them.

Rounding the next corner they saw the roof of a wayside building nestling amid the trees. "There may be a phone here," said Stepan, lengthening his stride. The others did their best to keep up.

As they neared the building a familiar figure stepped out from the shadow of a plane tree.

Kostya cried out in sheer disbelief. "*Peter!* How the devil did you —"

"It wasn't too difficult. I hadn't bargained for that fellow outside, but," he smiled, "you had neutralized him very effectively. He couldn't chase after me, and anyhow, he saw my gun."

Before that, Peter had used his weapon to hold back the men in the cave. They wouldn't know that he was now alone. He reckoned they'd wait a minute or so after his last shot, to make sure that there'd be no more. He'd made the most of that minute to get a start.

"I was some way up the mountain before they came out of the tunnel —"

"*Up?*" echoed Stepan.

"Of course. To go down was too obvious. I *started* downhill just to fool the man outside, but he couldn't move fast without his boots to check which way I'd really gone. So I doubled back and climbed above the tunnel again, and watched from above. Even if they'd glanced up, they wouldn't have seen me for the vines. While they were questing about in the wrong direction I ran along the terraces and cut down to the road as soon as it looked safe. I wanted to intercept you before you did anything silly."

"Silly?" Again Stepan could only echo him.

"Unwise. Unnecessary. Like rushing off to the police."

"I should have thought that was the most sensible thing to do," said Marina indignantly. "We thought you might be in awful danger. Surely, even now, we must —"

"Wait. We're a bit conspicuous here." Peter drew them into the shade from which he had just emerged. "Though I don't think they'd dare try anything on the open road – even if they recognized us – and only that look-out man has really had a clear sight of us."

"And *he* won't get far until he's found his boots," said Kostya with a chuckle.

"Why shouldn't we go to the police?" persisted Marina.

"Did you catch what those two men said, in the cave, about Shulgin?"

"Ye–es —"

"I get it," said Kostya quickly. "About protection? One was grumbling because Shulgin takes such a big cut out of their profits. So *he's* in on their racket – safely in the background. He fixes it so that the police turn a blind eye."

"Exactly. It's public knowledge now that there's been an immense amount of corruption in the police. They're cleaning it up as fast as they can. But before you go running to a policeman with a story like this, make sure he's straight. Or you could be in trouble yourself. Big trouble. It isn't just for the crooks that they can fix things," said Peter grimly, "they can fix *you* in a very nasty way."

Kate remembered that first morning at the police station, that horrible woman officer. *She'd* fix anybody she disliked, given half a chance.

"So we are to do nothing?" Marina was disgusted.

"For the time being, nothing," agreed Peter. "Except get back into town as quick as we can. We'll try for a lift, or there should be a bus soon. So – get back, take a shower, have a second breakfast, and make up on some sleep."

"I'll support that," said Kostya. "Especially the breakfast!"

THIRTEEN

Back in her cool bedroom at the sanatorium Kate slept off the night's exhaustion. When she surfaced and looked blearily at her watch, it was late afternoon.

A note in her father's scribble said: *Glad you're safely back! See you at dinner.*

"Safely back. . ." If he knew what real meaning lay behind those conventional words! But, as she dressed at leisure, she decided not to worry him with the full story of her adventures.

Some day perhaps, when they were truly "safely back" in England, she would tell him. Not now, though. She knew what this stay with Dr Yasnov meant to him. So much to discuss and compare, so many questions to ask and answer, in the brief time the two doctors had together. Her father needed a clear, untroubled mind to concentrate.

Next week Yasnov was taking him off to the conference in Odessa. She was glad now to know that he would not need her there. Accommodation was in great demand, and there'd be plenty of official interpreters around. She'd stay behind here, catch up on the typing and her own reading – have time too for her friends.

Only, as her father said jokingly, he trusted her not to "get into mischief". She wouldn't let him down. No more nocturnal excitements in the mountains, no more encounters with bootleggers. Just swimming and sightseeing.

Nothing could be more innocent than tomorrow's programme: tea with "Babushka", Stepan and Marina's grandmother. Babushka's memory went back so far, right beyond the Bolshevik Revolution of 1917. She had known the sanatorium when it was the Grand Duke's home. When little more than a child she had worked there as nurserymaid.

"You'll find her fascinating," Marina promised. "She is, of course, a little old-fashioned."

Kate took the hint and put on a dress, very crisp and clean. Even the young men smartened themselves up. Peter, surprisingly, had accepted the invitation to come along. Much more surprisingly, he had shaved off his dreadful beard. He pretended to have done so in Babushka's honour, but Kate wondered.

He seemed a different person. She could have passed him in the street unrecognized. Of course, when a person had some outstanding feature – like a half-grown beard – that was what you noticed and remembered. Take it away and you found a stranger, a face you had to learn all over again.

Peter no longer looked like a pirate. His smooth, ordinary features would have fitted into any bank or office. Was he still carrying the gun he had drawn from under his armpit the other night? She dared not ask. And there was another question that she still less dared to ask him: had he sacrificed his beard in case, by bad luck, he ran into the one bootlegger, the look-out man, who had seen him clearly by daylight?

That was an uncomfortable thought. The man had seen all of them, briefly, and he had most reason to remember Stepan who had knocked him down. There was a risk, a slight risk, for anyone of them. But *we* haven't any beards to shave off, she thought half-humorously. Still, it was a million-to-one chance against meeting that particular bootlegger amid the milling throngs of Yalta. She put the thought from her and determined to enjoy her afternoon.

Maria Ushinskaya – whom she was soon calling "Babushka" as the others did – was a tiny old lady, wrinkled as a walnut and much the same colour. She sat waiting to greet them on the verandah of her cottage. The painted woodwork might have been cut into its decorative patterns with a fretsaw. The steep garden sloped down behind to beehives and hen-coops under an apple tree.

Babushka's gnarled hands were folded over an apron as smooth and white as a swan's plumage. "Good afternoon, Mees Holford," she croaked, and then cackled with amusement at managing the English words.

"How are you? This *is* kind of you," said Kate. To save the old woman further effort she switched to Russian.

The faded eyes opened wider and positively twinkled. "You speak our language?" Again the delighted cackle. "That was something that Mees

Woolley could never do!"

Miss Woolley had been the English governess to the Grand Duke's children. She ruled the nursery with a firm hand, and Babushka, in those days a peasant girl of thirteen, had to fly to do her bidding. But, as the governess never mastered more than a few phrases of Russian, her young pupils had to translate her orders.

"They, of course, were supposed to speak English all the time in the nursery. When they went downstairs to their parents in the drawing-room it was more often French. The great ones never spoke Russian together." Babushka snorted. "They thought it was an uncivilized language, fit only for servants. And, of course, they did not want us to know what they were saying to each other! Oh dear, I am forgetting my manners, Katrina Ivanovna – you will take a cup of tea? Mees Woolley always liked her cup of tea. Marina, my dear, will you attend to the samovar?"

This, thought Kate, was almost too good to be true. She was going to witness the old ritual of tea-making with a samovar, something straight out of the vanished world of old Russia. It would be like stepping back, in England, into the age of Dickens or the Brontës.

Marina went into the dark cottage and emerged with a pot-bellied little copper urn, its polished curves winking in the afternoon sun. At its base was a tiny grate, with a vertical chimney rising through the middle of the urn and coming out of the top.

Stepan was sent down the garden to fetch fresh

water from the pump. Marina took pine-cones from a basket and dropped them down the chimney one by one. Then, when she had filled the samovar with water, she struck a match and kindled a miniature fire of pine splinters in the grate below. A bright flame shot up the chimney, the pine-cones caught, and the air filled with a resinous fragrance.

Soon the water in the urn was bubbling noisily. Marina took the teapot – which looked absurdly small for a party of six – spooned in some tea, and filled it with boiling water from a tap at the base of the urn. Then she placed it on top of the samovar to keep hot.

"Don't forget the food, dear. The boys will be hungry."

There were plates of little honey-cakes and other delicacies. For each person there was a dish of jam, but nothing to spread it on. Watching the others, Kate saw that most of them placed a spoonful of jam in their tea instead of sugar. There was no milk. Yalta being in the subtropical zone, there were slices of lemon, so often unobtainable in the cities of the north.

"Cups for the ladies, glasses for the gentlemen," said Babushka approvingly. "That is correct. It was always so. Now tell me, Katrina Ivanovna, do you too like Surbiton?"

Kate was floored by this unexpected question. She had never set foot in Surbiton, knew only that it was a south London suburb, very much like others.

"I – I believe it is very nice," she stammered.

"Mees Woolley spoke much of her home in Surbiton. I heard the name often on her lips, though the children had to tell me afterwards what she was saying. Mees Woolley spoke of it as a most wonderful quarter of London, a little English paradise. She pronounced the name with such feeling – I had not thought that the reserved British had such powerful emotions. Sur–bit–on, she would say, ah, Sur–bit–on!"

Kate almost choked over her tea. But, of course, it was so understandable. Poor Miss Woolley! Before the Revolution there must have been scores of English governesses like her, impoverished gentlewomen, without training or qualifications to earn a living, with nothing to sell but their refined English accent, so prized by the Russian nobility. How homesick they must have been sometimes, poor dears, shut up in nurseries and schoolrooms with a gaggle of foreign kids! No wonder Miss Woolley had looked back on Surbiton as her paradise lost.

"I hope that she saw her home again," said Babushka wistfully. "She stayed with the Grand Duchess, so bravely, to the last. When the Reds arrived, most of the rich people were taken off by your British warships – they fled to Paris, or England, or America. Mees Woolley must be dead now, God rest her soul. But I often wonder about those children. If I am still alive, perhaps they too . . ."

Once the old woman was launched on these reminiscences, there was no stopping her, and no one wished to. It was just what Kate had hoped for – to meet someone with eyewitness memories of Russia in the days of the last Tsar. She was relieved to see that Kostya and Peter were just as rapt. Even Marina and Stepan, who must have heard it all many times before, beamed approval and egged her on.

It squared, of course, with what Kate had heard: the modern young Russians wanted to know more about the recent past. For too long there had been an official conspiracy of silence about the happier side of life before Communism. Nowadays the lid was off.

For Kate Babushka's descriptions had a particular interest. They centred in the mansion that was now the sanatorium and in those ornamental grounds where she walked every day. Babushka brought it all to life again, peopling the stage with the shadows of the dead. She could recall even the day when the Tsar and Tsarina had come over, with the imperial children – Anastasia and the rest of them – from their summer palace at Livadia.

A shadow passed across Babushka's ancient face. "All dead now," she whispered. "All murdered."

Her cheerful humour returned as she switched to more amusing recollections. "Oh, the Grand Duke and his statues! Anything antique, no matter how damaged!" She remembered even the stone anchor. "That old stone with the hole in it? So that's what it was? An *anchor*?" Her laughter became almost uncontrollable. "My grandfather was one of the men who hauled it up there. He was one of the workmen on the estate. His language! Such a weight it was! And no beauty in it like the gods and goddesses, just an ugly lump of stone. But there, the Grand Duke wanted it, so up it had to come."

"Up?" said Kate. "From the bathing-place, you mean?"

"Yes, my dear. A fisherman had seen it lying on the bottom of the sea. So my poor grandfather and the other men had to get it out of the water and lug it up all those steps. Yes, life was hard in those days. The workers had to do whatever the great ones wanted."

"It's a beautiful spot, isn't it? The bathing-place."

"I expect so. I have never seen it."

"Never?" Kate was incredulous.

"No servant was allowed to go down the Grand Duke's Staircase – except a footman, say, or a valet."

"Why ever not?"

Babushka cackled. "In those days the gentlemen wore no bathing costumes. They were as bare as the ancient statues."

Tea over, she rose creakily from her chair and insisted on showing Kate the inside of her cottage. There was a gilded icon on the wall, a candle burning to light up the Virgin Mary's face. Seventy years of atheist government had not budged the old woman from her childhood faith.

At a word from his grandmother, Stepan took down a balalaika from the wall, and, back on the verandah, they gathered round him as he sat on the steps, cradling the triangular guitar and strumming an old folk-tune on its three strings. They clustered round and started singing. Kate knew some of the songs herself and was able to join in. Babushka became ecstatic at this. Her faded eyes filled with tears.

At last they had to say their goodbyes and start down the dusty lane to the town below. "It's been a wonderful afternoon," said Kate fervently.

"I should like to swim in the Grand Duke's bathing-place," said Kostya. "Do you think, Kate, if I promised to bring my trunks . . .?"

"I don't see why not. I'm sure Dr Yasnov wouldn't mind. He only asked me not to swim there alone."

"Let's all go," said Marina. "One gets so tired of the public beaches."

"Yes, one feels like a chunk of meat laid out on the butcher's slab," said Kostya.

So it was agreed to make up a swimming party for the following afternoon.

FOURTEEN

The visit to the cove was such a success that they repeated it several times.

It was a refreshing change to get away from the Yalta crowds – to plunge straight into its cool turquoise depths instead of picking their way across all those white pebbles. Stepan said he would like to hire snorkel equipment and explore the cove more thoroughly.

For the two Ushinskys these visits also provided an excuse for strolling past the mansion where Babushka had once been nurserymaid. They could report to her that there were now countless children, often from the poorest families, playing in the grounds that in her day had been enjoyed only by the offspring of the nobility.

Marina would point to some splendid exotic tree. "To think," she would say, "our great-great-grandfather may have had a hand in planting that!"

"I expect they let him dig the hole," said Kostya teasingly. He had no great respect for the old aristocracy. "Ordinary people have as many ancestors as a tsar or an imperial royal highness," he pointed out. "They just don't know all the names and dates, that's all."

Only on their third visit were Kate's friends challenged as trespassers. Needless to say, it was by Olga.

She was marching importantly between two

buildings, a number of medical files tucked under her arm. She paused, and beckoned Kate aside with her usual prim expression.

"These persons, Miss Holford . . ."

"They're friends of mine."

"I know – I have seen them with you before." Olga always managed to invest the simplest remark with a flavour of sourness. "But they have no business with the sanatorium? They have no relatives to visit?"

"No." She'll never forgive me, thought Kate, for that first morning.

"These grounds are not a public park. You may not understand – as a foreigner. It would not do if the whole population of Yalta —"

"Of course not," Kate nodded, but stood firm.

"I do not think the Director would be pleased if he knew."

"The Director does know. I told him before he went off to Odessa. I may ask any friends of mine here while I am his guest. So you might say," Kate concluded sweetly, "that they have permission – from the highest authority."

Olga looked daggers. "The Director is very easy-going. Some say *too* easygoing."

"I'm sure they do."

Olga stalked away. Kostya was grinning from ear to ear. "I know her type. A bureaucrat. We still have a lot of them – too many."

Olga was not the only person who noticed the comings and goings of Kate's visitors. It was on the fourth occasion, as they were lounging on the smooth rock slabs at the base of the cliffs, and

132

Stepan was unpacking the two snorkel kits he had hired, that Peter remarked quietly, "Don't look now, but I think someone up there is watching us."

"Marina." Kate stretched out her hand. "I saw a little mirror in your bag?"

"Certainly. Here you are."

Still on her back, apparently staring at the sky, Kate tilted the mirror so that it reflected, bit by bit, the cliff staircase as it zigzagged down behind her. She was relieved, and not altogether surprised, when the glass picked up a familiar little face peering from behind a rock.

She sprang up and turned. "*Ben!* You young monkey!"

The boy rose and began to descend the steps.

"Stay where you are! I told you never to come down here."

He ignored her order. She had to admit that, though his movements were awkward, he managed remarkably well.

"I must apologize for my bad manners," he said humbly as he joined them. She could almost hear his father speaking. The others smiled. She, feeling responsible for him, could not help sounding cross.

"You're very naughty. I told you to stay where you were."

"But I was more than half-way down. It seemed safer to continue. Now I shall not have to climb back by myself."

"But the other day, when we came here, you promised not to follow me down these steps!"

"I kept my promise. But that was the other day. This time you did not bring me, I came by myself. And so —" He shrugged his skinny shoulders, gesturing like a little old man. "Dr Yasnov says he wants us all to learn to be independent."

"Did he say that to you personally?"

"No," he conceded. "There was no need."

Kostya burst out laughing. "You can't win, Kate."

"This child," said Peter, "will make a good lawyer. Or perhaps a foreign minister. And run rings round them all at the United Nations."

It seemed best to let him stay with them. Then, when they left, they could see him safely up the cliff and back to the sanatorium.

They slipped off their clothes to swim. Stepan laid out the snorkel kit. It looked much the same as one Kate remembered trying herself. A mask covering eyes and nose, with a transparent face-plate for maximum vision; a plastic air-tube, shaped like a letter J, with a mouthpiece at the curved end; and two fins with stiff blades and soft shoes to fit over the feet.

Kostya was especially taken with the fins. "I shall look like a giant frog!" he exclaimed delightedly. All his swimming had been done in the rivers or shallow lakes of the north, so he had no experience of snorkeling and was eager to try.

Stepan gave him careful instructions. "You don't use your arms in swimming – the fins give you all the motive power you need, so you have your hands free to pick things up – sea shells, sea-weed —"

"Or any stone anchors I see lying about!"

"Oh, yes, don't leave them behind!"

Kostya was disappointed to learn that the snorkel did not give one any longer under water than a normal dive. "Only the duration of an ordinary deep breath? What's the point, then?"

Stepan explained patiently. With the mask protecting your eyes you could see more clearly. Before you actually dived you could float face downwards on the surface and take a leisurely look at what you were aiming for. Your face would be underwater but the snorkel tube would be sticking out above and supplying you with fresh air until the last moment before you dived. After that – well, you'd have free hands and clear vision until you had to come up for air.

"I'm afraid that if you expect to go wandering about under water for a quarter of an hour or so," he concluded, "you'll need aqualung equipment – harness, a heavy cylinder on your back, a weight-belt, the lot! Sorry, we can't run to that sort of thing."

"I'd like to see Olga's face," said Kate, "if she spotted us carrying all that through the grounds!"

Kostya settled for a first lesson in simple snorkeling. Stepan saw that his mask was properly fitted, the strap adjusted, not too tight, and the tube in place in front of his ear.

"Don't dive in, or anything dramatic," he warned Kostya, "or you may pull your mask off! Get used to the feel of everything as you lie on the surface, and then do a gentle jack-knife – bend at the waist, so that the top half of you goes under, and then straighten your legs behind you. Just take two or three deep breaths before you go – don't overbreathe, it won't help. Above all, relax."

"How the devil can I relax? There's so much to remember!"

No one was surprised when, after three descents, Kostya announced firmly that he had had enough for today.

"You don't want to overdo it the first time," said Stepan tactfully. "Anyone else like a go?"

His sister shook her head emphatically. She had tried snorkeling before and was not an enthusiast. Peter at that moment was swimming about alone on the opposite side of the cove. Ben's eyes were pleading, but he knew that his chances were nil.

"Apart from anything else," said Stepan, "the mask and the fins would be far too big to fit you." It was a face-saving excuse, but they all knew – and no one more than Ben himself – that there could have been no question of his taking a turn.

That left only Kate. Seeing that there was no competition, she said, "*I'd* love to."

Stepan questioned her closely on her previous slight experience and on her fitness and general state of health. She answered with cheerful confidence, having in the past few months had a complete medical check-up including X-rays. To shorten the interrogation she glibly rattled off the points to be checked before snorkeling. "No high blood pressure, no epilepsy, no diabetes —"

"You have caught a doctor's daughter!" said Kostya with a chuckle. "You did not ask *me* all this – but perhaps you do not think my life is so valuable?"

"I do not suffer from hay fever," she continued remorselessly, "I have not at the moment a cold in the head, I have no blockage of the Eustachian tubes." She paused for breath.

"And your heart?" demanded Stepan, a twinkle in his blue eyes.

"My heart is fine, thank you very much!"

"I am satisfied," said Stepan solemnly.

"You damn well should be," said Kostya.

At last Kate was allowed to slip on her fins and, having tested the fit of her mask, place it snugly in position. Stepan watched her but did not intervene.

"You have been well instructed," said Kostya. "No doubt by that brother of yours?"

Kate quickly put in her mouthpiece with the rubber flange between her lips and gums, gripping the two small lugs between her teeth so that the mouthpiece could not slip out again. No one now could expect her to answer Kostya's sly question.

She would follow exactly the instructions Stepan had given Kostya – it was one way to support Stepan against his mocking friend. So she slid quietly into the water and floated face-downwards, the end of her snorkel tube rising like a little periscope above the surface. The water below was glassily transparent, a turquoise world. It must be three or four metres deep immediately below her, falling rapidly away to six, ten, perhaps even deeper further out.

It was all coming back to her, the knack she had acquired a year ago. It must be like cycling, you could not forget. The fin stroke must be a long slow crawl, with your legs bending only slightly at the knees and your toes pointing backwards. Arms straight at your sides or straight in front when you went down in your jack-knife dive. Except when you needed a hand to pinch your nose through the mask. You had to do that to clear your ears of pressure as you entered the deeper water.

Up there – on the surface, in the brilliant sunshine – the cove was beautiful. But there was another, subtler beauty in this blue water underworld. It was all so clear, viewed through the mask. The only thing was the distortion of distances. A submerged rock looked closer than it proved to be.

Stepan came gliding down beside her. He pointed a warning finger upwards. Her lungs were already telling her she mustn't stay down any longer. She turned and finned her way up. As she rose, she felt the greater buoyancy of her body as the depth lessened, so that she shot up faster and broke the surface into the dazzle of the sun.

"Bravo!" Marina applauded from the rocks. Peter and Kostya were clapping. But of the little boy there was no sign.

She disengaged her mouthpiece. "Where's Ben?" she cried in alarm.

Peter answered. "He's all right. The imp can swim like a fish. He's coming up now."

The grinning face surfaced thirty yards out in the cove. Ben spluttered, then called across in his shrill voice, "It's so beautiful down there!"

"You gave me such a fright," she shouted, "vanishing like that."

He swam across to her. "I am sorry. But I am quite good under water. My father used to say I was like a little submarine."

"I don't think you need worry about his lungs," said Peter quietly, "whatever else is the matter with him."

"It is as Stepan was telling Kostya," said the argumentative child. "Even with a snorkel you can stay down only as long as your breath lasts. Therefore, even without a snorkel, I can stay down as long as you can."

"Well, you're coming out now," said Kate decisively.

"Just once more," he begged. "There was something I saw. I *must* go down again. Just this once. I will be so careful."

"No, Ben —" But he had not waited for her answer. He was gone.

There was only one thing to do. She pulled on her mask again, took two deep breaths, and went after him. Below her she could see the pale body of the boy moving with slow-motion elegance as he glided down to the sea-bottom. This was a different part of the cove. The floor was sandy.

There was a shadowy pattern on that floor, a dark curving line upon the silver, wavering slightly with the tremor of the water that they disturbed. It was part of an oval, so extensive that the further side faded away beyond her vision. The line made a frame in which Ben, now scrabbling furiously at something, formed a picture until it was clouded over with drifting skeins of sand.

Kate finned down towards him. She was thankfully aware of Stepan close by. For herself, there was nothing she could do. Her breath wouldn't hold much longer. She must surface soon – or die. But thank God, the awful child had ceased his scrabbling. He flashed past her. She followed and emerged, gulping and panting in the blessed air.

The juvenile submarine was beside her, wide-grinned with triumph. "You came down! So you saw for yourself!"

For the moment she could not answer. She struck out for the rocks nearby, wearily hauled herself out. Stepan and Ben climbed up beside her.

"You saw?" demanded the boy impatiently.

"I only saw a kind of shadowy line under the sea."

"But there is a man!"

"A *man*?"

"He has a beard, and a sort of helmet —"

"What on earth —" she exclaimed in disbelief. This must be a child's romancing.

"It will need ropes and strong men." Ben was excited but practical. "You think I am playing a trick? Naturally I could not lift it. I could only bring this."

He held up something he was clutching. The

water dripped from it, flashing in the sun like a necklace of diamonds. It was the handle and broken neck of an earthenware jar. And, as he rubbed it vigorously to clear it of encrusted mud and sand, a circle of tiny nymphs and satyrs seemed to dance into view.

Only later did Kate learn that it was part of a black-glaze amphora, a Greek winejar from the fourth century BC.

FIFTEEN

Everyone came crowding round to examine the discovery. Everyone was eager to follow it up, but Peter had to admit that he had no real experience of underwater swimming, and neither Marina nor Kostya would have been much help at that depth.

Ben was rebellious when he was positively forbidden to go down again. Kate soothed him as tactfully as she could. "It's *your* find, of course it is. But you're a patient in the sanatorium – just imagine the outcry if anything went wrong. *We'd* all be in the most terrible trouble. You wouldn't want that?"

"No, Kate." But the liquid eyes looked moister than usual. "But can you find it without me?"

"We can try." She turned to Stepan. "Did you see it – like a shadow on the sea-bed? A great wavy oval? Ben was more or less in the middle."

"Ye–es. Now you mention it."

They donned their masks, swam out into the cove, and dived again. Down, down, fighting the buoyancy of the upper water, then more swiftly as the greater depth operated on their side.

Below her the shadowy line wavered. She finned towards the centre of the oval. Stepan was a little to her right.

Something dark was protruding from the sand. She headed for it, hand outstretched to clutch, but the deceptiveness of the mask made it look nearer than it was. She missed her objective, glided over it, had to turn back. She saw now that it was the handle of another amphora. It looked rather big – even if she got hold of it could she take it up to the surface with her?

When she got her fingers round the handle she could see that it was not so big after all. This time the trick of underwater vision had exaggerated its real size. She pulled it easily from the soft sand – it was a complete jar, unbroken. As she finned upwards she held it upside-down, so that the sand in it spilled out, trailing behind like a wreath of tawny mist.

Stepan's fair head surfaced a second or two later. He had brought nothing up with him, but he confirmed Ben's story of the bearded man.

"It is a statue," he reported to the others as he scrambled out. "Much of the figure is buried in the sand, but it must be life-size, or even a bit more. Not stone. Bronze."

"Bronze?" cried Kostya. "Would it survive under the sea?"

"It does," said Ben.

They examined Kate's jar. It was black-glazed, like Ben's fragment, but in perfect condition, without a chip. The painter had decorated it with the wine god in a chariot drawn by panthers, and here too was a band of grotesque capering satyrs with men's bearded faces but the shaggy haunches and hoofs of goats.

"We're obviously dealing with an ancient ship-wreck," said Stepan. "Hundreds – thousands – of years old."

"The one the anchor belonged to!" cried Ben.

"Very likely," Kate agreed. "It will take an expert to say if the dates fit."

"The whole thing," said Peter, "is a matter for experts."

They all agreed about that. Amateurs could ruin an archaeological find like this if they muddled the evidence before the experts got to it. "It is the same as in a detective story," said Peter. "One must not touch anything at the 'scene of the crime'."

They had not much choice, anyhow. If there was really a wrecked ship down there, it would take proper divers and equipment to bring its contents up to the light of day.

Stepan was certain it was a sunken ship. In size and shape that shadowy line on the sand matched those of an ancient merchantman. "It is the timber of the bulwarks just protruding," he said. "I am certain. I brushed it with my hand."

"Wouldn't the timber have rotted away long ago?" asked Peter.

"Not at that depth," Ben broke in irrepressibly. "Papa showed me in a museum. Pine, cypress, cedar – all in glass cases. But one must take great care when bringing wood up into the air or it dis-dis . . ."

"Disintegrates?" Marina suggested.

"Yes. So it must be treated in the lab."

"We shall be guided by you, professor," Kostya assured him solemnly.

The presence of a Greek ship here was easy to explain. The Greeks had founded colonies all round the Black Sea coast. They had traded for centuries with the Greek cities further west, Athens and Corinth and even Syracuse in Sicily.

"I expect this ship has been buried in the sand for centuries," said Kate, "and then some storm uncovered it – or a shift in sea currents, or something. That's how these old wrecks come to light."

"And no one would notice it anyhow," said Marina, "except in those years when the Grand Duke had his swimming parties."

"It couldn't have been visible then," said her brother, "or the fishermen who spotted the anchor would have done some more searching. I know there weren't any snorkels then, but there were the old-fashioned diving suits. Anyway, sponge-divers can stay underwater for fantastic times without any apparatus."

"What do we do now?" asked Marina. "Who should we tell?"

Again they all felt reluctant to go to the police.

"Too much red tape," Kostya warned them. "We shall be stopped from swimming here. They'll ask lots of questions. How did we come to be here, when we have nothing to do with the sanatorium? Until Dr Yasnov comes back, it could be very uncomfortable for us. I know the police." He looked at Peter for support.

Peter said, "It would be quite correct if we waited and reported to Dr Yasnov. He *is* the Director. So, till he gets back from Odessa, we hold our tongues. And that includes you, Ben."

"My lips are sealed. Can I keep my bit of the amphora?"

They exchanged glances. Out of a whole ship's cargo that fragment could not matter much. Ben deserved something as a memento.

"I shall hide mine in my suitcase," Kate said, "and hand it over to Dr Yasnov. He'll see we've not been imagining things."

They got dressed. Mounting the steps, she thought she saw some improvement in Ben's agility. His handicap remained, but he seemed quicker, more vital. Perhaps this new excitement was giving him a psychological stimulus. He had taken a fancy to Kostya and chattered to him as they walked back.

Kate dropped behind with Stepan. "The cove is so beautiful," he said. "It must be wonderful by moonlight."

"Of course, I haven't been there so late."

"It will be some time before the next full moon. How much longer will you be staying here?"

"Two more weeks after Dad comes back from Odessa."

"So short a time?"

"Oh, look!" she exclaimed, not sorry to change the subject. "There's that awful woman again!"

They were nearing the mansion. Ben was looking round, waiting to say goodbye to them. Olga had appeared suddenly like a bad fairy. Her vibrant voice shattered the scented quiet of the gardens.

"Benjamin Shapiro! Where have you been, you bad boy? You have missed your session with the therapist!" With a glare at his companions she seized him by the ear and hustled him indoors.

"She should be ashamed of herself," said Kate. "She's not a nurse – thank God! – but even a secretary should know better than to grab a child's ear like that."

She avoided contact with Olga whenever possible, but the Holfords' mail went to Dr Yasnov's office and she had to collect it every morning. On the following day, Olga slapped the letters down with more than her usual curtness.

"You go swimming again today?"

"I'm not sure. Perhaps."

"I think you will not see your friend."

Kate misunderstood, and looked aghast. The "friend" most in her mind just then was Stepan. She had every hope of seeing him that afternoon. What could Olga know about *his* movements?

Olga went on maliciously. "You say the Director invited you to use the bathing-place? But I think even he would not approve that you took one of his patients to swim there."

"I didn't take him! Did he say I did?"

"He did not even say he had been there, deceitful child! But he boasted to another patient."

"And the other boy, of course, sneaked to you?"

"It was not another boy, it was a little girl. She very rightly felt it her duty to report the matter."

Kate saw it all. Ben was discreet enough. He knew he must keep quiet about his swim in the cove. But he *was* so young, and he'd badly wanted to impress the little girl. So, on impulse, he'd boasted as he wouldn't have done to the boys.

She just hoped he'd mentioned only the swim, not the wreck. After their decision to keep the secret until Dr Yasnov's return she felt pretty sure he would not have broken that promise.

Controlling her own temper with difficulty, Kate tried to smooth things over. "I didn't take Ben. He followed us without my knowledge. I didn't see why I should bring him straight back. We took care he should come to no harm – there were five of us – and then we saw him back safely."

"I know. I saw you." Olga sniffed. "So afterwards I put two and two together."

"I'm sure you did." Kate gathered up the mail and left.

For several days they did not revisit the cove. It was too tantalizing, wondering what secrets lurked there that they could not investigate further. One afternoon they took the water bus along the coast to visit Alupka. All they saw of the cove was the gash in the cliffs as they chugged by.

They saw too, further out in the open sea, the trim silhouette of the *Meltemi*.

"So your Americans are still around," said Marina. "Yalta is a good cruising base."

Kate laughed. "If Flann knew what *we* know, he'd be green with envy!"

Alupka was worth the trip. It was built partly in Moorish style, like a stage set for *The Arabian Nights*. Terraces and stairways covered steep slopes down to the sea. High above its domes and pinnacles the heights of Ai-Petri loomed like a cloud. This palace too had been the creation of a tsarist prince.

On the return journey Kate and Stepan leant on the rails and talked of other things.

"The day after tomorrow," said Stepan, trying to sound casual, "Kostya is taking Marina to the cinema. It's a film I've seen, and anyhow, a girl does not always want her brother around."

"No?" Kate hid a smile. It also worked the other way. "You'll have Peter," she said innocently.

"No, Peter's off on some business of his own."

"Do you think he has a girl somewhere?"

"If she's in Yalta, he could bring her along sometimes – she'd be welcome."

"Peter seems to be a law unto himself." She was tempted to mention Peter's gun. But something restrained her. She had a feeling that Stepan did not want to discuss Peter.

"He has his own interests," said Stepan. "But I don't think he'd find it very interesting to go down the Grand Duke's Staircase and see the cove under the stars."

"You don't?" Kate decided not to tease him any more. She said frankly, "*I* should."

Stepan squeezed her arm as it lay along the rail. "Then – as you say in English – may we 'make a date'?"

SIXTEEN

The evening was golden velvet – the same soft-
ness, the same glow.

Kate took her supper-tray to her father's balcony. During his absence Madame Yasnova had
twice given her dinner. But knowing that Kate
had her own friends now, typing for her father
and preparation for college, she did not intrude
upon her.

Even now, as she ate, Kate had Maxim Gorki's
Childhood beside her. She had to read it before
term began. Tonight it was hard to concentrate
on it.

Supper finished, she changed her skirt for
jeans, handier for clambering over rocks. First,
though, she slipped into her bikini. The walk
might end with a starlit swim. One never knew . . .

Stepan was waiting under the trees. It was not
late. The staff were still passing to and fro. For
once, thank goodness, no sign of Olga.

It was the first time they had been completely
alone together. At last she and Stepan could really
talk.

So, as they strolled through the gathering twilight, they discussed their futures. Stepan had
always thought of a job in Yalta. If he took a good
degree he would like to concentrate on the pests
and diseases affecting the vineyards. But he had
become less settled of late.

"I want to see the world first. Years ago it

would have been hopeless – ordinary people weren't allowed to travel. Now, we are hoping . . ."

Kate was not sure what she would do with her Russian degree. "I'm open-minded. It depends on . . . oh, so many things."

"Especially for a girl."

"But I'm like you. I want to see the world."

They talked of their families. A close-knit family sometimes made choices harder. He already knew a lot about her father. He wanted now to hear about her mother. Then he went on, "And your brother?"

She was taken off guard. "My *brother*?"

"That dear brother whose photo you showed us. The brother who, I feel sure, is *not* your brother."

She felt her face go hot, but the dusk hid that. She had better come clean about Henry, confess why, impulsively, she had stumbled into deception. "I – I didn't want any of you to get the wrong idea about him."

"But wasn't it the wrong idea?" he said teasingly. "For he was not your brother?"

"He's just a friend. Never anything more. Never could be."

"Excellent! In that case perhaps —"

She knew he was going to kiss her. And of course he did, drawing her to him with the hand he already held, his other hand suddenly firm and compelling on her shoulder-blades. She would always remember his first kiss, under the perfumed acacias. The scent of those trees would always bring it back.

They sauntered on, more slowly now, instinctively whispering though they had left the buildings far behind.

"I can't bear to think that you will be flying out of Moscow in three weeks," he said.

"Don't sound so tragic." She laced her fingers with his. "You're like a character from one of the great romantic classics! I must tell Peter, if you ask to borrow his gun, you're not to have it."

"Why should I commit suicide? I am very happy!"

"Fine. Remember, if we want to meet again —"

"*If!*" he cried, outraged.

"If," she repeated firmly. "You must be sensible."

"I don't want to be sensible!"

"Listen. It will be quite possible to meet again. I can come back to Russia. Honours students *have* to spend at least three months at a Russian university or polytechnic – they often spend longer."

Stepan brightened noticeably. "And I shall try to visit England," he promised.

They drew near the edge of the cliffs. The last gleam of daylight had gone from the western horizon. A dark sky arched over them, sequined with white stars. They saw the ancient anchor, pale in the gloom, at the forking of the paths.

"We should have brought a torch," she said.

"I'll see that you don't fall!" He cleared his throat. "Perhaps – perhaps you would like to swim?"

"Won't it be rather cold?"

"The cove is a suntrap all day. The surface

water should hold its heat."

"It *would* be nice to swim by starlight. Something to look back on."

As they reached the top of the steps he checked her with a sudden pressure on her arm. "Wait." His whisper was urgent. "I thought something moved."

They stood motionless. She could hear only the soft wish-wash of the sea lapping the rocks.

"My fancy, I think." She hoped so, too. She wanted nothing to break the spell.

They moved forward cautiously to the first turn in the staircase, where they could see down to the bottom.

"Damn!" he muttered.

There were lights bobbing below. Necklaces of golden reflections shimmered on the black water. Shadowy figures moved. There was a boat.

"What's happening?" she whispered.

"Someone's had a bright idea – maybe the doctors and nurses are having a midnight supper-party or something." Stepan's voice was sour with disappointment. "Why did they have to choose tonight?"

She was no less disappointed. They had never seen any evidence that the sanatorium staff used the cove. It was cruel luck that now, of all nights . . .

A voice floated up. Someone shouted, "Over here, I guess!"

"That's Flann!" she exclaimed, surprised. "I expect Mrs Hathaway fancied a barbecue. They've brought a boat-party from the yacht."

"It does not sound like a party."

Nor, she thought, did it look like one. All the dark figures appeared to be men. No pale dresses caught the beams of their lanterns. No high-pitched feminine voices or laughter echoed from the enclosing cliffs. Any barbecue held by Pearl Hathaway would have been a much livelier affair.

"Whatever they're doing," she said bitterly, "they've got here first. We'd better leave them to it."

"Not just yet. I'd like to know . . ."

For herself, she did not care. She wished they could creep away somewhere quietly. There was that summer-house where Dr Yasnov held his staff meetings. So long as they were together, and alone.

But Stepan's curiosity had been challenged by this upset in their programme. He had to find out.

"Wait. I'm going to see what they're doing."

"Oh, be careful . . ."

He had gone, stealthily merging into the gloom.

She sat on the topmost step, peering down. Again Flann's voice rang out, impatient, imperious. "Tell them to hitch the rope round it, the way they did last night."

Her heart sank in sudden dismay. Could it be – oh, no, it *couldn't* be! How could Flann possibly have heard about the wreck? But the boat had moved out into the middle of the cove. There seemed to be two men splashing about in the water near it, and one thing was certain – they were not swimming for pleasure. Their heads were covered by masks, and, worse still, they had big metal cylinders harnessed on their backs, wet

154

metal that gleamed in the lantern-light. She knew what that meant. They had aqualung equipment, they could get down to the wreck and stay there – and they had been down before tonight!

She counted five other men. Some of the voices seemed to be talking Russian. But, apart from Flann's shouted instructions, they mostly went about their work in a businesslike silence.

Kate's brain was racing wildly. Her first instinct – the obvious one – was to hurry down the steps and warn Flann that *they* were the first discoverers of the sunken ship. He must on no account touch anything without permission of the proper authorities.

A moment's thought made her hesitate. Would Flann take any notice? The "proper authorities" had not been informed yet. It looked suspiciously as though Flann was slipping in first, to loot the ship's contents before anyone could prevent him. There were, she knew, unscrupulous private collectors who would do such things. She knew nothing about Flann that would encourage her to trust him a yard further than she could throw him.

What would Stepan think? They must decide together on what was best to do. She could not bear to stay up here alone. Feeling every inch of the way with hand or foot, she crept down the rock staircase. At the bottom she found Stepan hunched behind a giant boulder. He turned his head as she knelt beside him. She felt his breath as he whispered in her ear.

"I think it is the statue they are trying to raise!"

155

They could see tantalizingly little. They had to keep their heads down. They could hear much grunting and muttered instructions. Now the boat was moving slowly through the water. Its side bumped softly against the rocks. The shadowy figures clustered round, strained, panted, heaved.

"You see, Mr Flann? It has been worth while!"

Kate knew that voice also. It was the deep bass of Anatoly Shulgin. She became even more mystified and now a little frightened too.

She peeped round the rim of the boulder. Yes, it was Shulgin all right. The lantern showed up his face, even the shaggy eyebrows, unmistakable. But her gaze was drawn to something else – something that was dull brownish green, encrusted after ages of immersion, but equally unmistakable. The life-size figure of a bearded warrior in a high-crested helmet.

"*Gee!*" Flann's gasp of awe was eloquent.

"It will clean up?" asked the Russian anxiously.

"Sure, it'll clean up." Flann laughed. "And so shall we!"

"It will sell for many dollars?"

"I'll say it will!" Flann was fingering the statue with reverence.

"How many dollars?" Shulgin demanded.

"Kinda hard to say. The marketing gotta be right."

"How?" Shulgin sounded greedily impatient.

"It's a new find. Gotta line up some experts to say it's genuine. No problem there – it is. But governments don't like stuff leavin' their territory.

They're apt to clap on an export ban."

"Moscow would," said Shulgin pessimistically.

"No problem, though!" Flann assured him heartily. "Not with the yacht. Then there's the sale. No public auction, o' course, no public anything. Leak the news discreetly. The right kinda collector – who's crazy to get hands on it and won't ask damfool questions. We'll get the dollars all right. Then I pay your share into a Swiss bank account – all top secret."

"I must be sure —"

"We've worked together a long time, Shulgin. Did I ever cheat you of your fair cut?"

"If you ever had, I should not have come to you with this information. If you ever had," Shulgin's tone was sinister, "you would not be still in business."

"Give me another day or two. There's a lot more down there. There's money even in the small stuff. Pottery, say, if it's like that sample bit the young woman brought you from the kid's locker."

So, thought Kate furiously, Olga had turned out Ben's locker, found the fragment of amphora – and run to show it to her idol, Shulgin.

"My divers tell me that there are hundreds of jars in the hold," said the Russian.

"You see? One might not fetch much. Chickenfeed. But hundreds! Too good to leave down there. But we'll need to work fast. That young woman won't have told anyone else?"

"No fear of that." From his voice Kate could imagine the smirk on Shulgin's face. "She will do

157

exactly as I told her."

"And the kid who found that bit?"

"He will keep silence. She has put the fear of God into him."

I can believe that, Kate told herself.

"OK. Let's get on. Barring any unforeseen hitches —"

Then came a hitch Flann could not possibly have foreseen. Kate was suddenly seized by an agonizing cramp in her left leg. She had to straighten it. Her shoe scraped noisily.

There was a startled outcry. A hand grabbed the collar of her denim jacket and jerked her savagely to her feet. She found herself looking down the barrel of Shulgin's gun.

SEVENTEEN

Flann swore. "We shoulda had a look-out!"

He stumbled across. Two silent shapes were there before him. They too held guns, pointed at Stepan. Kate saw their set faces in the lantern-light, expressionless as concrete. She did not like what she saw.

Flann cursed again, explosively, when he recognized her. "This has loused up everything! I know this girl. What's worse, she knows me." The full implications dawned upon him. "Worse still – a sight worse – she knows *you*!"

"That English girl? On your yacht that day?" He might be shaken, but Shulgin's voice remained cool. Its very calm was more alarming than Flann's furious dismay. He turned to Stepan and demanded in Russian, "Are there any more of you?"

"No."

Kate could have wished that Stepan had thought quickly enough to lie. Better to have kept Shulgin wondering.

Meanwhile, as he interrogated Stepan, she herself had to deal with Flann's questions.

"You and your boyfriend – Kate, isn't it? – too bad you happened to come down here just when you did! Now you'd best forget you seen anything, right? Anyways, you'd not want your pop to know what you were doin' with this Russki guy?"

A retort sprang to Kate's lips, but she did not utter it. Shulgin had turned to Flann.

"We take them to your yacht."

"Say —" Flann started to protest.

"We take them to your yacht. We decide then what we must do." He motioned her to the boat, bobbing gently on the black water. "Get in."

"I'll do no such thing!"

"Then we make you. Scream if you wish. Who will hear?"

Who would, in this cliff-encircled cove? Who would hear even a gun-shot?

One of the *Meltemi*'s crew – Zeki, she thought he was called – took his place at the outboard motor. She gave Stepan a swift questioning glance. His hands were fastened behind his back. He strained and writhed, but could only nod helplessly.

"We have no choice. But don't be frightened. They won't dare to hurt you – you've a British passport."

Zeki's dark arm reached out to help her. In the shifting beam of the lantern she read embarrassment in his look.

"Now you," Shulgin ordered Stepan. "And no funny business, young man! If the boat upsets you will be the first to drown. Which might not be such a bad idea! The handcuffs need not be mentioned in the official report."

Kate felt her flesh creep.

One of Shulgin's men sat down facing Stepan, pistol conspicuously ready. Shulgin and Flann stepped in. Shulgin turned to the divers. "The boat will come back for Yuri and the statue. When you have helped him with it, remove all traces here and make your way home independently. Mind you are not seen by anyone at the sanatorium."

One of the men began to voice a question, but Shulgin cut him short. "I cannot say at the moment if you will be needed tomorrow night. You will receive your instructions in the course of the day."

Zeki started the motor. If its gentle chugging was heard in the distance there was no reason why it should arouse anyone's suspicions. This coast, after all, was a holiday playground.

As they nosed their way out into the open sea Kate's mind flew back to that moment near the top of the Grand Duke's Staircase, when Stepan had fancied there was someone just in front. If only there had been! If only, as Flann had said, there had been a look-out! She and Stepan would never have been allowed to surprise the looters at their work, and they would not now be in this terrifying situation.

The *Meltemi* was anchored some distance out. Kate was helped aboard. Flann gripped her arm painfully and propelled her up the steps to the deck, then down below again into the saloon.

There sat Pearl Hathaway, elegant and expensive-looking even in her wrapper, a tumbler of whiskey beside her, a curl of cigarette smoke rising from her ring-laden fingers. Her eyes opened wide as the prisoners were brought down the companionway.

"Goodness! The British girl! What are *you* doing here?"

Before Kate could answer, Flann said roughly, "I could ask you the same. Thought you'da turned in by now."

"I told you before, honey. I don't sleep so good when you're out on these night jobs."

"Well, you can sleep now. You'd best go to the cabin."

"Not till I know what goes on," said Mrs Hathaway firmly.

"Maybe better you didn't."

Now that they were all down in the saloon, Stepan evidently thought it high time to say something himself. He burst out impetuously in Russian.

"Comrade Shulgin, I protest! I know that you are a very important person, but that does not give you the right to treat us like this. It is not permissible – not nowadays. I demand that this young British lady and I be put ashore —"

Shulgin's hand slammed brutally across his mouth. Kate cried out in horror. So did Mrs Hathaway. Stepan did not utter a sound.

"If you want more you can have it," Shulgin told him. "Or you can be gagged. But I'd sooner have you free to answer questions. Otherwise – understand that *I* do the talking." He turned to Flann, and said in his heavy English, "It is necessary we decide what to do. And quickly."

"It's this pair o' love-birds," Flann explained soothingly to Mrs Hathaway. "They stuck their noses in. Didn' mean to, but they did. Which is just too bad. Specially for them."

162

"They saw you at this shipwrecked galleon or whatever it is?"

"They sure did. It's not a galleon. I told ya. It's a real ancient Greek freighter from way back – several centuries BC, I'd reckon." Sensing that the Russian was becoming restive, he switched back to him. "OK, we gotta think fast. I'd have liked two or three more nights with those divers o' yours, but I reckon now —"

"You shall still have them. We must get everything of value."

"But – these two?" Flann scowled at the captives. His look of loathing – of frustrated greed – was frightening.

"Why should they ruin everything?"

"But we can't let 'em go!"

"No," Shulgin agreed. "Most certainly, it is not possible we let them go."

Mrs Hathaway broke in. "If you only need a few days clear, can't you lock 'em up in a cabin? If they're reported missing – if there's a lot of hoo-ha – well, Mr Shulgin's got his police contacts. He can fix things surely. They can stall long enough while you finish and we make our getaway." She turned to Kate. "Don't be scared. Nobody's going to hurt you."

"We don't have to let 'em go too quick," said Flann eagerly. "See here, Shulgin. We could hold 'em like Pearl says, then land 'em at some god-forsaken spot on the Turkish coast, where it'll take 'em another day or two to make contact with anyone —"

"Yes, yes," interrupted Shulgin impatiently,

"but sooner or later they tell their story. You have built up a profitable business in this region. Smuggling, black market, whatever pays best. If this story gets out, you are finished in all the Black Sea countries – not only the Soviet Union but Bulgaria, Romania, even your base in Turkey. You will not be able to show your face there again."

Now, thought Kate, the truth was coming out, the explanation of much that had puzzled her. It was obvious why Flann's professed enthusiasm for the ancient Greek legends was based on such little knowledge.

As if to confirm it, he let out a scornful laugh. "So what? I tell ya, Shulgin – I'm sick of your goddamn Black Sea. Once I've shifted this cargo, I'll be glad to quit. If all this antique junk fetches what I think it will, I'll be able to retire."

"And what about me?" Under those hairy brows, Shulgin's eyes were baleful.

"With your share, you can skip to the West. I know that's what you figure on doing eventually."

"When I am ready."

"Best be ready soon, then. Or these new guys in Moscow will catch up on you. That's the way I read the signs. From now on, corruption's out. The old bosses are being investigated. You been lucky so far. Get out while the goin's good."

The outboard engine could be heard again. There were voices at the landing-platform, grunts and thuds as something weighty was manhandled aboard.

"Hear that?" Flann was more self-assured now. "A few more boatloads, then it's up anchor, over to a quiet little place I know in Turkey, off-load again – an' we'll be laughin'."

The Russian shook his massive head stubbornly. "It is not how I planned to go. When I leave for the West I am not a man to crawl under barbed wire on a wet night. I must make dispositions in advance, get funds out of the country secretly beforehand."

"Sure," said Flann, "but you've no choice now. Once this story gets out, you're finished here. Just like I am."

Shulgin did not answer for a moment. In the silence Kate was conscious of the anchor coming up, the yacht's engines throbbing into life. When Shulgin spoke at last his words were quiet and cold, but the menace in them was all too clear.

"Suppose that the story does not get out?"

Kate looked around her wildly. Stepan, handcuffed, could do nothing. She could do nothing for him – except, if possible, escape and find help. The yacht was moving now, but the coast was still near, and though the cliffs might be impossible, a strong swimmer might be able to make it to the beaches near the town. If she had been on the open deck she would have tensed herself ready for the right moment and gone over the side. Down here in the saloon she hadn't a chance. Shulgin's silent henchman was watching. He'd be on her before she got a foot on the companionway.

There was a sudden interruption. A voice outside in the night, a distant voice amplified by a loud-hailer.

Shulgin's gun was instantly trained on Stepan. "One squeak out of you, young man!" he warned him. "Grigory!" he ordered the other Russian. "A gag!"

Grigory neatly lifted Mrs Hathaway's whiskey glass, swept the small tablecloth from under it, and rammed its folds roughly between Stepan's teeth. Stepan could only roll his eyes in helpless protest.

Zeki came pattering down from the deck. He faced Flann with a scared expression. "Sir! It is police!"

"Surely you can fix *them*?" Mrs Hathaway appealed to Shulgin.

He looked shaken. "I do not know *which* police. With some I have no influence. I must not be seen here. They must not come on board."

Voices continued in the darkness outside. Then the Turkish skipper came down with a look of alarm. "Mr Flann, sir! The police are not satisfied. They say we must turn and follow them into harbour."

"All right, Yusuf. Tell 'em you will. But hang on a moment," he looked at Shulgin, "I guess this is it. It was nice while it lasted. But . . ." There was a question in his eyes.

Shulgin swallowed. "You are right. It is time to go."

Now it was Flann who took charge. Kate saw a new strength and decision in the little man.

"OK, Yusuf. Tell 'em we will. Pretend to follow, but take an extra wide sweep round the headland, like you wanted a clear run in to harbour. Only –

don't run in. Swing to starboard, and head for the open sea. Like a bat outa hell. We gotta reach in'ernational waters before they catch us."

"Sir!" said Yusuf, and went. The loud-hailer continued its instructions for another minute.

"Damnation," said Shulgin regretfully. "Such a beautiful longterm plan I had made."

EIGHTEEN

"I'd best see what goes on," said Flann.

Shulgin followed him, asking anxious questions about the yacht's maximum speed.

The man Grigory took a chair facing the captives, his gun ready to hand.

Mrs Hathaway gave Kate a sympathetic glance. "You'll be OK. Not to worry." She looked dubiously at Grigory. "I'm going to put some more clothes on. Looks like it'll be one of those nights." She paused in her doorway. "I'd ask you into the cabin, honey, only this thug mightn't like it. But if you want the toilet," she pointed to a door at the foot of the companionway, "I guess even he's human enough to let you go in there."

"Thank you." For the moment it was the least of Kate's anxieties.

Mrs Hathaway came back to fetch her half-finished whiskey. "You'll be OK," she repeated, but did not sound too confident. The cabin door closed behind her. Kate and Stepan were alone – except for Grigory.

He watched them, silent and alert. He growled a warning when she removed Stepan's gag. She swung round and surprised even herself with her fiery stream of Russian.

"It's not necessary now – who is to hear? Do you want him to choke? Are you a savage or what?"

Grigory shrugged his shoulders. The yacht was

now swinging round, the floor slanted under their feet. Then, as it levelled again, the vibration accelerated, the vessel bucked slightly as it surged forward through the waves. They were racing now for the open sea.

Kate turned again to Stepan. "Oh, your poor mouth! It's bleeding. That monster!"

"It's nothing," he assured her, but he winced at her impulsive kiss. They sat close on the padded bench. She slipped her hand behind his back – Grigory was instantly on guard – but she was merely interlacing her fingers with Stepan's, gaining comfort and striving to give it.

"We have been unlucky," he whispered. "I cannot understand how this happened."

"I can."

She had learnt more in the cove than he had, as Shulgin and Flann had been talking in English.

"It was poor little Ben," she explained. "He'd promised not to tell anyone about the wreck – and he didn't, really. But he boasted to some little girl about swimming there – it was a chance to impress her. I don't think he has many friends among the other children. The girl sneaked to Olga – I expect the little toad will *be* another Olga when she grows up! Then Olga went prying in Ben's locker and saw that piece of pottery. Whereupon she rushes off to Shulgin – anything to curry favour with the great man!"

"I see now. And he turns at once to the American – because of the yacht."

"Did you understand what they were saying just now?"

"Not much." He smiled apologetically. "You know my English."

She explained hurriedly in a low voice. Grigory watched them balefully but did not intervene.

Flann's cruising was a cover for a variety of illegal activities in the countries bordering the Black Sea. To extend them into Soviet territory needed an accomplice like Shulgin in a high position with official influence.

"You don't surprise me," said Stepan. "He's into everything. I've heard stories, but it didn't do to repeat them. Police corruption, shady deals in factories – and we found out ourselves about the liquor racket. And Flann gives him a secret link with the West."

And, now that government investigations were beginning to expose such people, Shulgin had been wisely starting to plan his escape to the West. In his own good time, not at a moment's notice. But with their stumbling on his operations in the cove – and now, by a lucky chance, this challenge from a policeboat – Shulgin might have to get out quickly.

"What happens now?" she whispered anxiously.

"Depends on the speed of the yacht – and the police launch. If it overtakes us in coastal waters we'll have to stop, or they'll open fire. Then, if they board us, we'll see if he can talk his way out. Depends whether the man in command is a Shulgin man or not. *We* shall take a bit of explaining away. You especially."

"Because I'm British?"

"That's it. I'm only an unknown Soviet citizen.

170

Years ago, I'd have been easy to deal with. Scared into silence – or just . . . silenced. He might still be able to fix it."

"You mean —" Her eyes were big with horror. "Kill you?"

"There used to be lots of handy official excuses. Died in custody, shot while attempting escape, that sort of thing. Much harder to fix nowadays, though. He can't be very confident himself, or he wouldn't be making a bolt for it." He pressed her hand to encourage her. "You're my best protection. He can't silence *you*. And if anything happened to you it would be headline news, because you're a foreigner. It would be handled at top level in Moscow. Investigators would be sent down here. And the last thing he wants is Moscow investigators."

"I hope you're right." Her voice trembled. She was close to tears. She could think of nothing more to say. She could only hold, awkwardly, one of the hands manacled behind his back.

Flann and Shulgin came below again looking more cheerful. Mrs Hathaway emerged from the cabin, fully dressed and made up.

"Relax, honey," said Flann. "It's all gonna be OK."

"You're sure, Mike?" She pleaded for reassurance.

"Sure. Yusuf fooled the cops – they went through the harbour-entrance before they realized we were veering out to the open sea. This yacht can move. Once we're out of territorial waters they can't touch us."

"What about Mr Shulgin? And his . . ." she hesitated, searching for a word, "his colleagues," she ended with disdain.

"We got all that figured out." Flann poured whiskey as the two men settled themselves in cane chairs. "Once we've shaken them off, once we're safe in in'ernational waters, Shulgin will take our boat and slip ashore some quiet place along the coast."

"Won't he have some awkward questions to answer?" She did not sound as though she minded if he did.

Flann chuckled. "If Mr Shulgin wasn't good at answerin' awkward questions he wouldn'ta got where he has."

"And what about Kate? And this good-looking Russian boyfriend of hers?"

This time there was less assurance in his answer. "They sure are a problem. For Shulgin. We'd best leave it to him to solve in his own way," he said evasively.

"I thought we could drop them off in Turkey or some place?"

"He reckons they know too much. He needs six months clear, to tidy up his affairs and make his getaway."

"Six *months*? They can't be kept hidden all *that* time."

"Sure they can't."

"You've got something nasty planned. Come clean, Mike."

"See here, honey – if you'd only keep your pretty nose outa this! Like I said, it's a problem

172

for our friend. He'll handle it without us. They'll go in the boat with him. The less we know the better."

Kate could sit quiet no longer. She leapt to her feet and assailed Shulgin vehemently in her best Russian. Grigory jumped up, but Shulgin waved him back.

"What are you planning to do with us?" she demanded. She forgot how Stepan had been dealt with, but the big Russian made no move to strike her. He eyed her with his cold unnerving stare. "*I* can't disappear without trace," she reminded him. "My father is an important man. The sanatorium will find my bed hasn't been slept in, I'll be reported missing. The British ambassador will be brought into it. You'll have stirred up a hornets' nest. They won't let up till I'm found."

He heard her out. Then he said, smiling, "Quite so. And no doubt you will be found, very soon. And your ambassador will have nothing to protest about. Young people have drowning accidents in any country."

"Drowning accidents?" she faltered.

He nodded. "It is sad, but often it happens on holiday. A girl and her boyfriend go for a midnight swim. They are swept out to sea. But the sea brings their bodies back to the beach – or some fisherman finds them, floating."

He meant it, no doubt of that. Pale, she swung round on Flann. "You know what he's saying?"

Flann avoided her blazing eyes. "I don't get all this Russian."

"But you know – because he's already told you.

173

He's going to throw us overboard!"

Mrs Hathaway screamed. Flann, glad of an excuse to turn away from Kate's accusing fury, tried to pacify her. "I warned you, honey - you an' me gotta keep out of this. Why not go back to the cabin and lie down? Hey, have a drink —"

"You've mixed me up in a lot of things but you're not going to mix me up in murder!"

"Maybe this kid's just gettin' hysterical. See here, go to the cabin, take a tablet - you've had no sleep —"

"Nobody's had any sleep!"

"I give you my word. When you wake up, it'll be daylight, all these folk'll be gone, it'll seem like a nasty dream."

"Mike! You must *do* something."

"What can I do? There's three o' these Russian guys. They all got guns, they're desperate. We gotta let 'em handle it their way."

Mrs Hathaway opened her mouth to argue but there was an interruption. Shulgin's other aide came thudding down the companionway and muttered something in his ear. Shulgin looked relieved as he interpreted to Flann.

"Yuri says that the police launch is a long way behind. And Yusuf tells him that in five minutes we shall be out of territorial waters. They cannot possibly overtake us in that time."

"Great! That's real great. It's all gonna work out, honey. Our friend will be able to slip back and no one any the wiser. An' *we* needn't ever come near this darned place again." The optimist in Flann reasserted itself. "The police won't ever know he's been on board."

During their wrangle Kate's imagination had been working fast. She could see all too clearly why Shulgin was so confident. She was picturing the headlines in the British press.

Holiday romance ends in tragedy

The body of Kate Holford, 17-year-old daughter of well-known London specialist, has been washed up on a beach in the Crimea. Miss Holford had apparently gone for a midnight swim with a young Russian she had met on holiday. The local police are satisfied that there are no suspicious circumstances.

No suspicious circumstances. . . How often she had read a news item ending with those words! And of course there would *be* no suspicious circumstances. Shulgin's men would see to that. No wounds, no marks of violence. Stepan's handcuffs would be removed at the last moment. How pleased they would be to find she was wearing a bikini under her jeans – it would be supporting evidence for the official story!

Suddenly there was a new sound. A deafening noise overhead.

"What's that?" screamed Mrs Hathaway.

Before Flann answered her Kate had recognized the sound. It was a helicopter.

If it had been the beating of angels' wings it could not have been more welcome.

NINETEEN

Yuri and Grigory came down, their usual wooden features showing acute anxiety. Yuri gave the bad news.

"He says there is a police helicopter," Shulgin explained. "They are hovering over us. They say, stop or we open fire."

"You can't stop – not now!" wailed Mrs Hathaway. Her instinct for self-preservation overcame her concern for the young captives. "I tell you, Mike, I'd die if they put me in one of their Russian cells." She appealed to Shulgin. "You and your men have got guns. Can't you show some spunk and —"

"Have sense!" Flann interrupted curtly. "They can't fight a helicopter with handguns."

"If we start shooting, it will only confirm their suspicions," said Shulgin. "They will be justified in following us beyond the territorial limit – they will radio the launch, they will bring up any other help they need. Someone will come on board, that is certain."

"They mustn't find *you* here."

"No, it is better I face them." Shulgin spoke rapidly. "They will be surprised, yes. But they are accustomed to treating me with respect. If I say that I was already carrying out my own investigation of your activities – if I say that they may have spoilt everything by blundering in like this," Shulgin smiled as the ingenious excuses developed in his mind, "we may see some nervous faces, much embarrassment, apologies . . ."

"Maybe – but you still gotta explain *these* two! They'll have plenty to say."

The yacht was slowing down. Yusuf had not waited for Flann's instructions. It was not only Mrs Hathaway who had a healthy instinct for self-preservation.

"We lock them in a cabin." Shulgin snapped out an order. His men went into action.

Kate's scream was stifled by a dusty cloth crumpled and shoved between her lips. Her hands were wrenched behind her, she felt cold metal as the handcuffs clicked round her wrists. In the background Mrs Hathaway was gabbling. "Do be quick – but don't hurt her!"

The two men moved with deft precision, as though this was a drill they were accustomed to. Another cabin door was flung open, she was thrown on a bunk, and, almost before she could start to kick, her ankles were bound tightly to the rail.

Looking sideways she saw that Yuri, with some help from Shulgin, was stretching Stepan on the bunk opposite. They had gagged him again. His blue eyes rolled with helpless, voiceless rage.

The three men went out. A key clicked in the lock.

The yacht had stopped. It rolled gently. The helicopter was no longer deafening. The noise came and went as it circled the vessel.

A clamour of excited voices overhead showed that someone had landed on the deck. Then came a little procession of booted feet descending the companionway. Now the newcomers were in the saloon, just outside the door.

Kate writhed on the blankets. Never mind the gag, never mind the handcuffs – if only she could pull her legs free, swing them off the bunk, and kick the door. But it was no good. Yuri and Grigory knew their job.

Stepan too was struggling, his face flushed with effort, his breath coming in tormented gasps.

She stopped, exhausted, and lay still, straining to catch the conversation outside.

Shulgin was at his most aggressive. She could imagine his expression as he confronted the astonished police.

"You did not expect to find *me* here!"

"No, Comrade Shulgin. I was told to pursue this vessel because it had disobeyed an order to return to harbour. We had to scramble and take off —"

"I congratulate you on your promptness." Shulgin spoke with elaborate sarcasm. "You may have ruined everything by your interference. As it happens, I am myself conducting an investigation into this yacht and its activities."

"No one told me —"

"No one knew," said Shulgin grandly. "It is a top-level matter. That is why I took personal charge. If I discover anything of a criminal nature I shall of course hand over the evidence to your superiors."

He emphasized that last word cruelly. Kate could not help admiring the man's self-assurance.

He's going to get away with this, she thought despairingly, they're all so scared of him.

Shulgin pressed his advantage. "It was I, in fact, who instructed the captain to ignore the instructions from the launch. I did not want my inquiries interrupted. As you see, I have two of my own men with me. I am in full control of this vessel. I hope that satisfies you."

"Not entirely, Comrade Shulgin." The police officer sounded surprisingly resolute. Oh, *good*, thought Kate, the man's standing up to him. "I was told one other thing – that there are two persons held on board against their will. Can you tell me anything about that?"

Shulgin snorted. "What a fantastic idea! Of course not. There is Mr Flann, and this American lady, Mrs Hathaway, and a Turkish crew of three."

"These two persons were abducted within the last hour or two."

If anyone was genuinely amazed it was Kate herself. How had the police got on to this so quickly? She listened intently for Shulgin's reply.

He laughed. "Have you anything to support this preposterous story?"

A quiet voice intervened. "There was an eyewitness."

Kate's heart seemed to jump. Surely she knew that voice? But until it spoke again she could not identify it for certain.

Shulgin was blustering but not beaten. "Who is this individual? He's not even in uniform. He looks like some scruffy layabout off the beach."

"He showed me his credentials." It was the police-officer now who sounded confident. "He is an investigator from Moscow, a detective."

"A *chief* detective," the new voice corrected him politely.

It *was* Peter, Kate realized exultantly, Peter the Pirate! She was not mistaken. So Stepan had been right – there *had* been someone else moving stealthily in the darkness on the cliffs.

Shulgin was still desperately struggling against the net that was closing in on him. "You can't be a chief detective – you are too young."

She heard one of Peter's rare chuckles. "Promotion has been quicker lately. There have been many unexpected vacancies. But if you doubt my authority, here are my papers."

For a minute or two only a confused murmur could be heard through the cabin door. Then Shulgin said, in a voice Kate could hardly recognize, "I can explain everything."

"There will be quite a lot to explain." Peter seemed now to have taken control. "I have been down here for almost three months. A very pleasant summer assignment! A whole team of us have been investigating your manifold activities. When it comes to court it will make a fascinating story – and by staging tonight's little melodrama you provided us with a fitting climax. And the best excuse I could have wished for to take immediate action against you! No, Shulgin!" Peter's level tone changed suddenly. It was like the crack of a whiplash. "Drop that gun! You others, likewise. Now, Mr Flann, if you will kindly open these doors."

The last remark was in very passable English. And he never let on to me that he knew a word, thought Kate afterwards. But at the time she was so overjoyed to hear the lock click and see Peter smiling down at her that she could not feel indignant.

"You are not hurt, Miss Holford?" he inquired formally. The policemen behind him could not see his wink. He had whipped the gag from her mouth. Someone was unfastening her handcuffs.

By the time she and Stepan were sitting in the saloon again the yacht was trembling under their feet as the engines were restarted. The dawn showed through the portholes as they swung round and headed for the harbour.

"You will have to make a statement, and sign it," Peter told them. "But it can wait until you have had some sleep."

Once safe ashore, she declined his offer of a police car. She did not want to startle the sanatorium at that early hour. Stepan took her there by taxi.

She was fast asleep in her room when the maid came on duty, so that her "disappearance" was never reported. It remained an untold story until her father and Dr Yasnov returned from Odessa that evening.

TWENTY

The bigger story – the exposure of Anatoly Shulgin's complex network of crimes – Kate was able to read at home months later, when his trial in Moscow won headlines and lengthy coverage in newspapers all over the world.

Under the harsher old regime his activities would have earned him the death-penalty if they had been uncovered, although probably they would not have been. As things were now, his life was spared but he was condemned to a long prison sentence.

Another news story reported fully in the foreign press was the raising of the ancient ship and its cargo from the seabed. That took a long time, what with the patient procedures of the archaeologists and the preservative treatment of the timbers in the laboratory. It was two years before the skeleton vessel and its contents were on display in a specially built museum.

Kate was able to visit it on one of her study courses in Russia before finishing her degree. It was exciting to see everything set out in glass cases – the now-shining bronze statues, the swords and daggers and spearheads, the gold and jewellery, pendants and bracelets and medallions, a great ram's head drinking cup, and hundreds of homelier objects, bowls and plates and storage jars. There were chisels and other tools, even traces of the foodstuffs carried more than two thousand years ago, almond shells and olive stones and spices.

Especially thrilling was the notice, printed in half a dozen languages, recording the circumstances of the discovery.

"Look!" cried Ben excitedly, pointing to the top line. "They have put *my* name first – Benjamin Shapiro!" He had grown a lot in the two years and had been able to leave the sanatorium with his disability almost cured. He was no longer a "little imp", but an imp he remained, and always would.

Stepan was there too, of course. Kate had seen him the previous year also, and the bond between them had strengthened. He was hoping next year to come to England and visit her in her own home.

Her name followed Ben's on the museum notice. Then came Stepan and Marina Ushinsky and Kostya Komarov.

"Why have they left out Peter?" Ben demanded indignantly.

Stepan laughed. "That's Peter all over. He never liked publicity."

And he quietly entwined his fingers with Kate's, as he had often done before. Somehow, she never got tired of it.

THE HAUNTED SAND

Hugh Scott

"Murder, Frisby! Murder on the beach!"

There's something creepy in the churchyard. There's something deathly down on the sand. Darren feels it, Frisby hears it, George thinks it's a bit of a laugh. But there's nothing funny about murder…

"Intriguing ingredients abound: a haunted church; fearful chases; ghostly weeping; skulls; bronze helmets; gems and The Black Death… Rendellesque subtleties of storyline build to an unforeseen climax."
The Times Educational Supplement

THICKER THAN WATER

Penelope Farmer

"Help me," the voice said. "Help me."

Becky and Will are cousins. But apart from blood ties they seem to have little in common: Will, skinny and withdrawn; Becky, plump and forthright. So when Will comes to live with her family in the heart of Derbyshire mining country, Becky is hardly overjoyed. What's more, it soon becomes clear that something disturbing is haunting Will...

"Striking and well-conceived ... with a fitting and very moving climax... Bears comparison with the best of her early books, *Charlotte Sometimes*."
The Times Literary Supplement

"Penelope Farmer's gripping tale of supernatural possession is as convincing as it is genuinely frightening."
Scotland on Sunday

SHADOW OF THE WALL

Christa Laird

"There's only one way which is reasonably safe, Misha, and it's not very pleasant." Misha sat back on the pile of newspapers... Sheer physical panic seized him, beginning in his feet and rising up like an electric current through his limbs.

"Not ... the sewers?" he croaked.

It's spring 1942, and life in the Warsaw ghetto is hard and often brutal, with the Jews subject to beatings and execution at the hands of the hated SS. Young Misha lives at the Orphans' Home run by the heroic Dr Korczak. But the time is fast approaching when Misha must prove himself a hero too...

"A story full of excitement and compassion."
Geoffrey Trease,
The Times Educational Supplement

"A book to make you cry."
Jessica Yates, The Daily Telegraph

GOING UP
Peter Hunt

For Tom Rowlands and Sue Marriot the time has finally come... They're going up! What's it like at university? Is it really all rave-ups and rag weeks? What about work? Follow Tom and Sue through their first year at college – making friends, joining societies (or not), hunting for digs, frequenting cafés, going to parties, nursing hangovers, taking exams and generally experiencing the whole mixed bag of university life.

"Tells more about college life than any well-intentioned student guide." *The Guardian*

"An attractive larger-than-student-life account, almost a teenagers' Tom Sharpe in the sustained wit of the dialogue."
The Times Educational Supplement

THE CHARLIE BARBER TREATMENT
Carole Lloyd

How do you cope with a death in the family? Some people break down; others, like fifteen-year-old Simon Walters, clam up. Friends, family, neighbours – all are given the same cold shoulder. Somehow, though, shaking off a complete stranger proves a lot more difficult. But then, as Simon quickly discovers, Charlie Barber is someone very special.

"Exceptionally powerful and original."
Kaye Webb, Books

THE LAST CHILDREN

Gudrun Pausewang

It's the beginning of the summer holidays and the Bennewitzs are on their way to visit grandparents in the mountains. Suddenly, there's a blinding light in the sky – and the Bennewitzs are on the road to hell...

Shocking, distressing, brutally honest, this book has already profoundly affected thousands of readers in Germany. Read it and it will change you too.

"This disturbing book shouldn't be limited to the teenage market but should be compulsory reading for most adults, especially those in positions of power."
Judy Allen, The Sunday Times

MORE WALKER PAPERBACKS

For You to Enjoy